ROBOTS RULE!

BATTLE
OF
THE
BOTS

To Amy,

An editor of many gifts, talents, and skills,

Thanks for everything,

From the bottom of our lithium batteries

With special thanks to Brandon Robshaw

Copyright © 2015 by Working Partners Limited
Series created by Working Partners Limited

www.hmhco.com

Text set in Adobe Garamond

The Library of Congress has cataloged the hardcover edition as follows:
Richards, C. J., author.
Battle of the bots / C.J. Richards ; illustrations by Goro Fujita.
p. cm. — (Robots rule! ; 3)
Summary: The evil Dr. Micron is in jail, but the scandal at TinkerTech has caused a lot of anti-robot feeling in Terabyte Heights, making life difficult for the ten-year-old robotics genius George Gearing and his robot buddy, Jackbot—especially since Micron is the only person who can help George restore his parents, and his price is a jail-break.
1. Robots—Juvenile fiction. 2. Scientists—Juvenile fiction. 3. Friendship—Juvenile fiction. [1. Science fiction. 2. Robots—Fiction. 3. Friendship—Fiction.] I. Fujita, Goro (Artist), illustrator. II. Title. III. Series: Richards, C. J. Robots rule! ; 3.
PZ7.R37856Bat 2015
813.6—dc23
[Fic]
2014044085

ISBN: 978-0-544-33932-3 paper over board
ISBN: 978-0-544-93524-2 paperback

Manufactured in the United States of America
DOC 10 9 8 7 6 5 4 3 2 1
4500645823

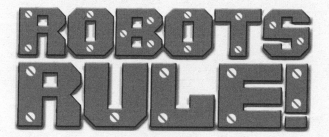

BATTLE OF THE BOTS

C. J. Richards

Illustrations by Goro Fujita

Houghton Mifflin Harcourt
Boston   New York

ROBOTS RULE!

BATTLE
OF
THE
BOTS

1

It was a beautiful Saturday morning in Terabyte Heights. Birds sang in the trees, and sunlight beamed through the kitchen window on George Gearing and Jackbot, who sat together at the breakfast table, playing a lively game of User-Virus-Firewall.

George whipped his hand out from behind his back, curled into a claw to represent Virus. Jackbot's metal pincer whirled around at the same instant, holding up a cardboard cutout of a hand with all five fingers straight up.

"Firewall blocks Virus!" Jackbot crowed. "I win!"

"All right, all right," George said. "One more time!"

I bet he'll do Firewall again, George thought. *He*

probably thinks I won't expect it because he's just done it. I'll get him with User!

He thrust his hand out, two fingers pointing down like little legs—only to see Jackbot turn around holding the cardboard cutout of the claw hand.

"Ha!" Jackbot cried. "Virus annoys User! I am the champion!" Jackbot did a victory dance around the kitchen and bowed to his imaginary fans. "Want to go again? Best out of thirty?"

"No, thanks," George said, sagging into his chair. "I think I've had enough humiliating defeats for one day."

"Hey, it's not my fault you made me a genius," Jackbot said.

From the other side of the table, Uncle Otto looked up at them with a scowl. "Could you two please stop bickering and give me a little peace and quiet?" he asked. "I'm trying to concentrate here!"

Otto was hunched over, holding a small electric motor in one hand while carefully loosening the tiny casing screws with the screwdriver attachment of his robotic arm. It had been several weeks since Otto had been released from the hospital, and he was finally getting used to his new prosthetic.

"Couldn't you fix that later, when we get to the junkyard?" George asked.

"I could," Otto replied, not taking his eyes off his work. "But this is the motor for the air conditioning unit in the truck, and it's supposed to be hot today."

George smirked. That wasn't the only reason his uncle couldn't resist tinkering. Otto had always distrusted modern technology, but once he'd been fitted with his new arm, things had changed. Otto loved it and all of its various attachments. He used them every chance he got.

George rose from the table to grab a glass of orange juice and a couple slices of bread. He turned to Jackbot and held out the bread in front of him. "Will you do the honors?" George asked.

But before Jackbot could answer, Otto reached over and grabbed the bread from George. "Allow me!" he said. Otto squeezed his eyes shut, concentrating hard. A moment later, the screwdriver attachment in his arm retracted, and was instantly replaced by a blowtorch. Grinning with pride, Otto then proceeded to wave the blowtorch over the slices of bread in a complex design. Finally, he handed the toasted bread back to George with a flourish. "There you go, kid! Eat up!"

George studied the design on the toast, puzzled. "Is it supposed to be a dinosaur?"

"Or perhaps an ancient Viking rune of some sort?" Jackbot guessed.

Otto glowered at them. "It's a smiley face, you bone-heads! Gee, talk about giving a guy a hard time . . ."

George grinned and took a huge bite of toast. "It's perfect, Otto," he said through a mouthful. "Thanks."

"Say it, don't spray it," Jackbot said, holding up his Firewall hand to block the crumbs.

Just then the doorbell rang. George zigzagged around Mr. Egg and the dishwasher-bot, who were bustling around in the kitchen, ran down the hallway, and opened the door. He found his elderly neighbor, Mrs. Glitch, standing there. Her gray curly hair sprung out from her head in an even wilder fashion than usual, like a star going supernova. Her eyes looked puffy and red, as if she had been crying. A robot with a TV screen for a head stood by her side. George knew the robot well—it was Hector Protector, Mrs. Glitch's glitchy security-bot.

"Good morning," George said. "Is everything all right? Does HP need fixing again?" The old robot was always breaking down in weird ways—a couple of months ago he had started hanging upside down from trees, and another time he had kept saying everything backwards. Each time, Mrs. Glitch had come to George for help.

"No, no, it's—it's not that," Mrs. Glitch said, shaking her head. "He's fine—just peachy. Aren't you, Hector?"

"I am fine," HP said expressionlessly. He'd been made before the voice intonation programs were improved. "How are you?"

"I'm, uh, great," George said, confused. "So . . . if nothing's wrong with HP, what can I do for you?"

Mrs. Glitch took a deep, steadying breath and said, "You have to take him, George. I can't keep him anymore."

George was shocked. "You're giving him up?" he exclaimed. "But you've had HP for years!"

"Seven years, two months, and twenty-one days," HP confirmed flatly.

"I don't *want* to get rid of him," Mrs. Glitch said, her voice quavering. "But I'm the only person on the block who still has a robot—besides you, George. People are starting to give me dirty looks! Everyone else has deactivated their bots. I mean, I can't really blame them. After what happened, how do we know that TinkerTech products are safe?"

"Of course they're safe!" George said. "Except when Dr. Micron made all the robots into crazed killers . . . and then when he turned the MOD devices into deadly mind-control machines . . ."

Mrs. Glitch raised an eyebrow. "Does that sound safe to you?"

"Well, no," George said. "But Micron's locked away in prison. With Professor Droid reinstated at TinkerTech, I bet everything will be back to normal in no time."

George sounded more confident than he felt. He'd been watching the news with everyone else during the last couple of weeks. Since the MOD debacle, TinkerTech had been shut down, and Professor Droid was under investigation by the police. It was all bad news for George—no TinkerTech meant no apprenticeship. Until everything blew over, George was stuck back in school.

Mrs. Glitch sighed. "I hope you're right, George, but until then, I have to get rid of Hector. And I can't bear to deactivate him. Could you look after him at the junkyard for me? I know he'll be safe there." She patted

HP's metal shoulder, her eyes watering once more. "Goodbye, Hector, my dear. Remember to install all of your updates, all right?"

"Glitch . . . Mrs. . . . goodbye," HP stammered. George looked at him in surprise. The stress of their separation must have been causing the robot to talk backwards again!

Mrs. Glitch choked back a sob and hurried away.

"You'd better come in," George said. He pulled HP inside, where all of George's house-bots—who had taken to hiding in the house since the anti-robot movement began—studied him curiously. "My uncle will take you to the junkyard in his truck."

"You . . . thank," said HP. He stepped into the hall and carefully wiped his big flat metal feet on the mat.

Within no time, George was rattling down the road in Otto's truck, with Jackbot and HP in the back seat. George had been going to the junkyard every day since finding out the truth about his parents and Project Mercury. He had spent nearly every waking minute down in their secret laboratory — or what was left of it — under the junkyard.

"So what are we supposed to do with this joker?" Otto asked, jerking his thumb at HP.

"Just keep him there until Mrs. Glitch is ready to take him back," said George. "He won't be any trouble."

"Hear that?" Otto said over his shoulder to the robot. "You're not gonna be any trouble, right?"

"Trouble any be not will I," said HP.

Jackbot looked at him curiously. "Why are you talking backwards?"

"Wrong gone has program speech my," said HP.

"Want me to fix it for you?" Jackbot asked.

"Point the what's," said HP.

As they drove along, George saw what had become of Terabyte Heights, and shook his head. The previously pristine sidewalks were piled high with stinking garbage, and all of the parks had become overgrown jungles. When TinkerTech closed, the municipal authority had deactivated all of the town robots, and now there was nobody to do their jobs. Robot-driven cars had been deactivated as well, and so the roads were clogged with human drivers who were seriously out of practice. As Otto's truck neared the center of town, traffic continued to worsen until the sound of blaring horns was deafening. Just as Otto's truck was about to cross an intersection, a car shot out in front of him, forcing him to slam on the brakes.

"Idiot!" shouted Otto, laying on the horn. "I never thought I'd say this," he grumbled, "but I'd be glad to see robots back on the road again!"

"Everything will be back to normal soon," George said. He realized he'd been saying that a lot lately. He hoped it was true.

"Hmm," said Otto, gazing at something through the driver's-side window. "I'm not so sure about that." George craned to see what his uncle was looking at, but as the truck passed through the stoplight, he could see the frightening sight all too clearly himself. The tall, gleaming structure of TinkerTech Headquarters came into view; its once packed parking lot was empty, except for a few patrol cars. Black and yellow police tape crisscrossed the entrance, and two tall men in dark suits and sunglasses guarded it. But that wasn't what Otto was looking at—TinkerTech had been a ghost town for a while now. The alarming thing was happening right in front of it.

At least a dozen people were marching outside the entrance, chanting, "Robots all must be destroyed! Jail for that Professor Droid!" and carrying signs that said things like TINKERTECH IS A TINKERWRECK!

George swallowed hard. "They look pretty upset, don't they?" he murmured.

"I'll say!" Otto agreed. The traffic ground to a halt at TinkerTech's front door.

A woman with flyaway red hair and big round glasses marched by Otto's truck, brandishing a sign that read ROBOTS? NO BOTS! She caught sight of Jackbot and HP in the back seat and shouted, "Hey—they've got robots in that truck!"

Within seconds, the demonstrators had surrounded them, banging on the sides of Otto's truck.

"Give us those robots!" the woman demanded. "Don't

you realize they're dangerous? They must be deactivated immediately!"

Otto rolled down the window. "Don't worry," he said, trying to sound calm. "I'm taking them to be scrapped at my junkyard."

"That me told nobody," said Hector.

"Shhh!" George said, putting a finger to his lips. "Worry don't. I mean, don't worry!"

"We'll scrap them for you!" the woman said. "Won't we, guys?"

The other marchers cheered, waving wrenches and hammers in the air. George peeked into the back of the truck. "How dare these people threaten us!" Jackbot said, indignant. "We are local celebrities! Heroes! Paragons of virtue!" HP, on the other hand, looked terrified. He had wrapped his skinny metal arms around Jackbot's head, and was chanting, "Home like place no there's! Home like place no there's!" George looked back at the road. The vehicles had started to inch forward, but a line of protestors had planted themselves in front of the truck, barring the way.

"Okay," George said, thinking fast. "We need another way out of here, Jackbot—now!"

"Right," Jackbot said, extricating himself from HP's grip. "Activating GPS system. Alternate route found. Otto, reverse seventy-three yards, take your first right, and then a left after two hundred and eleven yards."

"Did you get that?" George asked, turning to his uncle.

"Got it!" Otto said, grinding the gears into reverse. The truck shot backwards, then left into a hidden driveway and out through a back alley.

George sighed with relief as the crowd of angry faces disappeared behind them. They sped out of the alleyway and found themselves on a small road that ran alongside the TinkerTech building.

"We did it!" George said. "We got away from those—"

The words died in his throat as a small army of soldiers ran onto the road from all sides. Once again the truck was surrounded. George's stomach lurched. Guns pointed at them from every direction.

A huge man in a green flak jacket shouted at them from the driver's side. "Stop! And put your hands up where I can see them!"

George and Otto put their hands in the air, and Jackbot and HP raised their pincers. "It seems we have jumped out of the frying pan and into the fire," Jackbot said.

"Shut it, tin can!" Otto barked out of the side of his mouth. Then he cleared his throat and addressed the soldier in a friendly voice. "What seems to be the problem, Mr., um . . . ?" He squinted at the soldier's nameplate pinned to his chest. "Surge?"

"That's Sergeant Surge to you!" the man sneered. "You have trespassed into a restricted area. Identify yourselves immediately or you will be detained!"

"Oh—uh, all right," Otto stammered. "I'm Otto

Fender, junkyard owner and automobile repairman. I'm on my way to the yard now—took a wrong turn."

"A likely story," the sergeant muttered. "How about you?" he snarled, pointing at George.

"George Gearing. I'm just a kid."

"Just a kid?" Jackbot said, poking his head up into the front of the truck. "Don't be so modest! This here 'kid' is a technological genius, not to mention a local hero! And, I might add, a pretty decent basketball player."

George tried to elbow Jackbot to get him to be quiet, but it was too late. "And what are those?" Sergeant Surge asked, suspiciously.

Before Otto could answer, Jackbot had leaped onto Otto's lap and reached out the window to shake the sergeant's hand with his pincer. "Pleasure to meet you, sir —the name is Jackbot. Visionary, thespian, Casanova, warrior for peace . . . I could go on, Major—"

"Please don't," Otto muttered.

Sergeant Surge blinked. "I'm—I'm not a major," he said.

"Really?" Jackbot said, aghast. "Well, you certainly

should be. You have the stature of Julius Caesar himself!"

The sergeant appeared to blush. "Oh, that's very nice of you to say . . ."

"Not at all!" Jackbot said. "I'm a robot. I only speak the truth. And the truth is, we really did take a wrong turn. It was an innocent mistake."

Sergeant Surge looked from Jackbot back to Otto, then gave a curt nod. He took a few steps back from the truck and called out to his unit. "It's all right, men. Fall back. Let's let these good people get on their way."

George slumped down in his seat with relief as the soldiers waved them through.

"I did good, didn't I, Otto?" Jackbot said, still sitting on the big man's lap.

"Yeah, you did all right, tin can," Otto answered with a smirk.

"Well, here we are," Otto said as they pulled up to the junkyard's front gate.

Through the truck's windshield, George could see a

crowd of robots milling around outside Otto's Grotto: tall, elegant butler-bots and maid-bots, squat gardener-bots, grease-splattered cook-bots, robots of every size and shape. They all turned and stared at Otto's truck.

"More?" Otto spluttered. "I don't have enough room for the ones I have—how am I going to take these in?"

Mrs. Glitch wasn't the only person in town too soft-hearted to deactivate her personal bot. For the last week or so, people all over Terabyte Heights had been abandoning their robots in front of Otto's junkyard, in hopes that they could stay there until the anti-robot sentiment died down. The junkyard had morphed into a robot refugee camp.

"Aw, but you can't just leave them there," Jackbot said. "Look at them!"

The robots *did* look pitiful. They gazed at George and Otto with glowing eyes that blinked at them slowly.

Otto sighed. "Oh, all right. What's a few dozen more robots in the yard . . ."

George grinned and jumped down from the cab. "Don't worry, robots, you're welcome here!"

The robots responded with a chorus of bleeps and a rainbow of blinking lights.

Otto hopped out of the truck and dragged open the gate, and all the robots scurried into the safety of the junkyard.

At first the yard looked empty, but soon robot faces began peeping out from behind piles of scrap and from inside battered old smart cars. Within moments, the whole place was buzzing, all of them bleeping and clicking and talking so loudly that Jackbot had to bang on a trash barrel with a sledgehammer to get their attention.

"Listen up, new guys!" Jackbot shouted. "This is Otto's junkyard, so he's the boss!" Jackbot turned to Otto. "Go ahead, Otto, tell them what to do! They're robots—if they aren't given orders, they get a little funny in the head."

Otto looked out on the sea of metal faces, then around at the junkyard. George followed his gaze. Since the abandoned robots had started arriving, the junkyard had never looked cleaner. Junk was organized by type into neat piles, and the walls of the little shed, which served as Otto's office, were bright with a new coat of paint. "Um," Otto mumbled, "Jackbot, why don't you take charge, eh?" He turned to the other robots. "Y'hear that? You gotta do whatever this little tin can says, okay?"

Jackbot's green eyes glowed brightly. "Me? Why . . . I've never been in charge of anything before. I can feel the power surging through my transistors! I, Jackbot, leader of bots! Master of the junkyard! Commander of the—"

"Don't get ahead of yourself," Otto muttered. "Just keep them out of my way. Clear?"

"Crystal," said Jackbot.

Otto turned to George as they both walked farther into the junkyard. "So, what's the plan for today?" Otto said. "Or do I even need to ask?"

In the far corner of the yard, George could see the silver hatch that led down to his parents' secret Mercury Lab. The ground around it was still blackened from the fire that started during their last confrontation with the evil Dr. Micron. "I'm getting close to fixing the device," he said. "I know it!"

"Sure, sure," said Otto carefully. He pushed out his lower lip, as he often did when he was absolutely *not* sure about something. "But, did you ever think of taking a break, kid? You've been down in that hole for two weeks straight. A boy your age needs a little time for other things, like friends, school, sunlight . . . you know, stuff like that."

"A *break?*" George sputtered, stopping suddenly. "How can I take a break when Mom and Dad are floating around in a computer network as ones and zeros? I'm the only one who can bring them back! If I fail—" He didn't want to think about the end of that sentence.

"Look," Otto said, scuffing the dusty ground with his boot. "I think you've put a little too much pressure on yourself. When your parents left you that message about saving them, they didn't know that the whole lab had already gone up in flames." He looked up at George, his eyes soft. "You've been trying your very best—but the machine self-destructed. You can't blame yourself for that. And if you can't get them back—"

"I gotta go," George said shortly. He didn't want to hear any more. He was wasting time. "See you later." And before Otto could say another word, George ran off, past the teams of busy robots and the tottering heaps of rusty old junk, all the way to the metal hatch. He tugged the hatch aside easily—it had been warped by the heat of the explosion—to reveal a flight of metal steps leading down into blackness. He felt a familiar warmth against his leg, and pulled from his pocket the blue marble his dad had given him back when he was little. The marble that had started this whole journey into the secret of Project Mercury, that had contained the message from his parents, telling George that they weren't dead after all. It glowed with a comforting blue light, as if his parents were telling him, "Go on. You can do this. We believe in you."

Taking a deep breath, George descended carefully down the dark stairs, the marble lighting his way. At the bottom, he flicked the switch Otto had installed. Fluorescent tubes flickered on and drenched the remains of his parents' lab in bright light. It still hurt him to see the blackened ruin, but luckily the firefighter-bots had extinguished the flames before everything was destroyed. The power booster, the electro-oscillator, the recoding unit, the molecular analysis device, and the conversion chamber had all been heavily damaged—and there was nothing whatsoever left of the quantum particle accelerator. But thanks to its reinforced titanium casing, the central computer core—the machine that held his parents' data—was still intact.

The task was clear: replace all these incredibly complex

pieces of highly specialized equipment with bits of junk from his uncle's junkyard. How hard could that be?

On a scale of one to ten? Probably about twelve. Give or take a million.

George grabbed a cardboard box brimming with some of the stuff he'd been gathering from the yard: copper cables, assorted batteries, old silicon chips, a thermometer, a microwave oven, a primitive 3-D printer, and about seventy-five soda cans. He studied the Project Mercury plans that he'd spread out on a table—the ones Jackbot had found in his parents' computer file. George had printed them out poster-size and had been using them to rebuild the machines. The only problem was, many of the components were things he had never seen or heard of before, so figuring out what they did and finding replacements for them had been an agonizing process.

He'd managed to rig up a basic power supply for the central computer and construct a makeshift conversion chamber out of the hull of an old speedboat. But there was still so much to do. George weighed some of the old batteries in his hand. *Maybe I'll work on the power booster today*, he thought to himself. *If I could link these batteries together so they all charge each other in a continuous loop, that might be enough . . .* He began connecting the batteries using old jumper cables, and immediately became absorbed in his work.

Five minutes—or maybe five hours?—later, the silence of the lab was broken by a voice. "Hey, Robot Boy. What's cooking?"

George turned around to see his friend Anne Droid, her smile framed by pale blond hair. Sparky, her dog-bot, sat on his haunches beside her, his silicon tail wagging.

"Anne!" George said. "I didn't hear you come in!"

"Are you kidding me?" she said. "I bet the people down the street heard us come in. Sparky knocked an entire box of wrenches down the stairs! You must have been on another planet."

"Yeah," George said, looking down at the batteries. "I guess I was."

Anne looked her friend up and down, and crossed her arms over her chest. "How long have you been below ground, George? You look terrible."

George rubbed his eyes. "I don't know. Not long," he said.

"Hmph," Anne huffed. "Too long, if you ask me. Do you even remember who I am? Anne, your best friend? Who you haven't seen since the second digital revolution?"

"Oh, come on," George argued. "It hasn't been *that* long!" Though it was true he hadn't seen or spoken to Anne for at least a week. He'd been spending every moment he could down here, even getting Otto to write sick notes to school for him so he could work in the lab. George looked around, desperate to change the subject. "Hey, Sparky!" he finally said, walking over to the robot dog and patting him on the head. "How are you, boy?"

Anne grinned down at her pet. "He's okay. Dad keeps

telling me to leave him at home, with all the anti-robot people around, but I don't care about them. Sparky stays with me no matter what."

"How is your dad?" George asked.

Anne's smile faded. Professor Droid, head of TinkerTech, was now Public Enemy Number One. "Not great," she said. "The cops are still questioning him every day. They don't believe that he didn't know how dangerous Micron's MODs were. They figure he's the head of TinkerTech, so how could he *not* have known?"

"Why can't they understand that it wasn't his fault?" George protested. "He was a victim of Micron's mind control plot just like everyone else who was wearing the MOD!"

"I've told you why: the town needs someone to blame," Anne replied sadly. "And Dad isn't exactly defending himself, because he feels responsible for what happened." She looked down at the ground. "Last night at dinner he said that once the police are finished questioning him, he might sell the company and move away. Start over somewhere else."

"What?" George exclaimed. "But—Terabyte Heights would be lost without TinkerTech!"

"Maybe," Anne said. "But he won't listen to me."

A heavy silence stretched between the two friends. George's gaze drifted to the batteries. They were all dead, of course. But if he could get the biggest one juiced up —it had belonged to a tractor—maybe he could use it to charge the others . . .

"It would be awful if I had to move away," Anne finally said. Sparky whined at her feet, sensing the sorrow in her voice. "I grew up in this town."

"Yeah," said George, still distracted by the power booster puzzle. He picked up the tractor battery and heaved it onto a worktable. "Shame it's such an old model," he mumbled to himself. "But in principle, this should—"

"George!" Anne said. "Are you even listening to me?"

"Of course I am!" George replied. But within moments he had turned his attention again to his work, and began searching for the positive and negative terminals to a jumper cable. "What were you saying?"

"Maybe I should come back when you're not busy," Anne said. Her voice was strained, but George was too caught up in his work to notice.

"Actually, that would be great," he said, not looking up. "Thanks, Anne!"

"Come on, Sparky," she muttered, walking back up the metal stairs.

"Bye!" George called after them. But Anne said nothing as she closed the hatch behind her.

Did I do something wrong? George wondered. Sure, he could have paid closer attention to what Anne was trying to say, but his work was too important. *I'll call her later,* he promised himself, and linked up the cables to the big battery.

George worked through the day. He forgot about lunch. He forgot about everything except trying to get Project Mercury back online.

He had a good idea of how to make a power booster that would supply enough energy to convert streams of data into living biomatter. But then he still had to finish up the electro-oscillator, fine-tune the new recod-ing unit, and run some tests on his molecular analysis device.

George sighed. His hands were covered with small burns and cuts, and his eyes were itchy and dry. But he couldn't take a break now, not when he still had so much left to do.

His thoughts were interrupted by the scrape of the hatch opening above him.

George covered his face with his hands. *Ugh! I forgot to call her!* he thought. "Hey, Anne," George called out. He rose from his worktable to turn and look at her. "Listen, I'm sorry about earlier, I just—"

"I am not Anne," said a deep electronic voice. A huge robot rolled forward into the light at the top of the steps. It had a rectangular mouth with big square iron teeth and flashing yellow eyes.

George's knees turned to water.

"I am the Caretaker," said the robot.

3

"No," George whispered. "It can't be ..."
Micron was in jail! What was his robotic assassin doing
here?

The Caretaker floated down the stairs on its powerful
thrusters, coming to rest a few feet from where George
stood. Its last command had been to kill George—it
was probably here to finish the job!

"I've defeated you before," George shouted, grabbing a hammer from the table beside him. "I can do it
again!" He flung the hammer as hard as he could, but
it bounced off the Caretaker's head with a clang. The
robot continued to advance as if nothing had happened.

George took a few steps back, frantically searching for another weapon. He scooped up a heavy metal

wrench that was lying on the floor and charged toward the Caretaker, hoping to smash the control panel in its chest.

But the robot's steel arm shot out and its pincer attachment seized George's neck and hoisted him into the air. George brought the wrench down as hard as he could on the Caretaker's head, but the other pincer swatted it away.

The Caretaker moved steadily forward, squeezing George's neck until his face turned red. George tried to scream, but his voice was barely a choked cry.

The robot stopped, eyes flashing as it made a series of clicking noises. *It's choosing which attachment to use,* George thought, feeling sick. *The drill? The circular saw?*

A thin tube appeared at the end of its free pincer. It pointed straight at George's head. *What is that?* George thought. *Some kind of laser gun?*

A moment later, a blazing red light glowed on the Caretaker's finger, illuminating George's face. *It's going to liquefy my brain!* George thought in a panic, pressing his eyes shut. But there was no pain. George opened his eyes to find that the light had been shut off.

Huh? George thought.

"Retinal scan complete," the Caretaker announced, dropping George in a wheezing heap onto the floor. "You are George Gearing, as advised."

George rubbed his sore neck. He was confused. "Of course I'm George Gearing!" he said. "Haven't you come here to kill me?"

"Negative," the Caretaker replied. "Killing, kidnapping, and all other excessive force programs have been temporarily suspended."

George crossed his arms. "Well, if you can't do any of those things, what *are* you good for?"

The Caretaker swapped its laser scanner for a mop head, and proceeded to clean up a bit of engine oil that had spilled onto the floor in front of its feet. Once it was finished, it played a tinny rendition of the *Nutcracker Suite*.

George blinked. "Right," he said. "Now I remember why I hate Tchaikovsky."

The Caretaker was silent.

"I don't get it," George said. "If you didn't come here to kill me—and I doubt you came just to disinfect my parents' lab—why are you here?"

"You have a call," the Caretaker said.

"A call?" George asked. "From who?"

The robot touched a button on its control panel, which flipped around to reveal an LCD display. After a moment's buffering, a familiar handsome face filled the screen.

"Hello, George," said Dr. Micron. "Surprised to see me?"

George opened his mouth but no sound came.

"You certainly look surprised," Dr. Micron said. "Come now, George. Surely you didn't think you'd seen the last of old Chip?"

George found his voice. "How are you doing this?" he blurted. "You're in jail!"

"Such trifles are nothing to a man of my genius," Dr. Micron scoffed. "Or perhaps you have already forgotten about my little winged friends?"

George's eyes widened. "A moth-bot," he said.

"Good to see you're sharp as ever, my boy," Micron said. "Yes, it flew quite easily through the ventilation system and into my cell while a guard was delivering breakfast this morning. I'm using its video capabilities to transmit this call through the Caretaker. Impressive, no?"

The moth-bot must have backed away, because the view panned out to show Micron in a cell, wearing an orange jumpsuit.

"Thrilling," George muttered. "So did you just call me to brag?"

"Not at all," Micron said. "I'd like to make you an offer."

Now it was George's turn to scoff. "Oh, really? What could you possibly have that I would want?"

Micron leaned closer to the camera, so that his face filled the entire screen. "Your parents," he said.

George's face fell. "What? What do you know about them?"

Micron smirked. "Ah-hah!" he chuckled. "All ears now, are we, Gearing? I know you've figured out that old Mom and Pop are alive inside Project Mercury—and from the looks of that mess behind you, you still haven't managed to restore them."

"I'm close," George countered. "I'll have them back any day now!"

Micron gave a short laugh. "That's optimistic of you, George," he said. "But do you really think an eleven-year-old boy can singlehandedly rebuild one of the most complex devices ever created with a dead battery and a bunch of soda cans?"

"So, what now?" George said, his voice faltering a bit. "*You're* going to help me?"

"That's right," Micron said with a smile. "You get me out of this cage—I'll help you get your parents back."

George was furious. After all Micron had done, did he actually expect George to break him out of prison? "You think I'd help you escape? I'm the one who put you in there in the first place!" he exclaimed. "No way, Micron. You're staying right where you are. Where you deserve to be!"

Dr. Micron nodded. "Okay, George. I thought you might feel that way. But if you change your mind, contact me here." An IP address flashed on the screen below Micron's neck. "Got that?"

George said nothing.

"Just remember," Micron said in a low voice. "I am the greatest computer engineer alive. If there's anyone who can fix that machine, it's me. So, good luck with the repairs. You'll need it."

The screen went black.

"My mission is now complete," the Caretaker announced. "Goodbye." George barely moved a muscle as the huge robot trundled back across the lab—picking up several pieces of assorted garbage on the way—and blasted its way up the steps and into the night.

George sat unmoving for many long minutes, thinking. He'd done the right thing. He was sure of that. But then, why did he feel so bad?

Because I could have gotten my parents back, he thought with longing. *Soon. Maybe even . . . tomorrow.* But at what price?

"Hey, George!" Otto was calling him from outside. "Quitting time! Last one to the truck is a faulty spark plug!"

"Okay, okay," shouted George. "I'm coming!" He cast a last look around the smoke-blackened lab, the floor strewn with tools and scrap. The half-rebuilt machines were scattered around the room, dark and silent.

George walked over to the batteries he'd been working on all day, and flipped a switch to test its power capacity. A second later, the power booster began to hum—first quietly, then louder, and louder, until the vibration of it rattled George's teeth. Suddenly a light above George's head shattered into a million pieces. George yelped and switched off the power.

I don't need Micron, George thought to himself, smiling in the dark. *Mom and Dad left that message because they believed in me—and I'm not going to let them down.*

George fought off the waves of sleep that threatened to overcome him. He was sitting in his history of technology class at school, the last lesson of the day, listening to Mrs. Hertz drone on about the Industrial Revolution. That morning, Otto had refused to allow him to call in sick to school again.

"You can't hide away in that lab every day," his uncle had said. "Go to school. See a few carbon-based life forms, for goodness' sake, instead of whiling away the hours with a bunch of talking tin cans!" George didn't have the energy to argue.

"When people talk about the Industrial Revolution," Mrs. Hertz was saying, pacing the room in her usual frenzied way, "they usually mean the development of steam-powered engines and mechanized industries during the early nineteenth century . . ."

George felt his eyes beginning to close. He wished Jackbot were there to take notes for him, but he didn't dare bring a robot to school anymore. Since the trouble with the MODs, most people who still had a robot left it at home, behind closed doors. Jackbot couldn't bear staying at home, so on the days when George went to school, the little robot accompanied Otto to the junkyard, to help Otto oversee all the bots that had been left there. At least with Otto, George could be sure Jackbot was safe from those anti-robot wackos.

Even Patricia Volt, who never left the house without a state-of-the-art android by her side, hadn't been seen with a robot in weeks. *Cookie must be climbing the walls without someone to groom,* George thought, thinking of Patricia's annoying little meBot. Without Cookie's company and constant pampering, Patricia looked depressed. She didn't seem to be listening to the teacher—instead, she was staring out the window with a miserable expression on her face. For the first time ever, George felt sorry for her. He knew what it was like to miss a robot friend.

"But that wasn't the only industrial revolution," Mrs. Hertz continued. "At the beginning of the twentieth century, the world turned to electrical power, and that change deserves to be called a revolution itself. It heralded the dawn of the advanced technological world we know today."

George stifled a yawn. *This is ancient history,* he thought. *What good is listening to it when I could be putting my family back together?*

He'd been down in the lab every evening for the past week, but last night he had suffered a major setback. He'd rebuilt every component and networked them to each other — except for the most important one, the central computer core. No matter what he tried, he couldn't successfully transfer the data to the conversion chamber in order to turn it into biomatter, a crucial step. His parents had developed a next-generation digital transmission device for the job, and it was the only part of the central computer that had been completely destroyed in the fire. He had scoured the Project Mercury schematics for its design, but it was nowhere to be found. George had spent days researching the newest forms of hyper-digital communication, but nothing had worked.

He put his head in his hands.

"George, you okay?" whispered Anne. True to his word, Professor Droid had enrolled Anne in Terabyte Heights Middle School after their first encounter with Micron. After seeing what Anne had done to booby-trap her bedroom, he figured a little time out of the house would do her good. Normally, George would have been thrilled to be in the same class with his best friend—but at the moment, he wasn't in the mood to talk to anyone.

"Yeah, sure," he mumbled, hoping she would take the hint.

She didn't. "Look, George," Anne murmured. "I know Project Mercury is important to you—but you're working yourself too hard. You look like a zombie! Like a really tired zombie."

"I'm not working hard enough!" George said. "I'm stuck."

"Well, sometimes if you walk away for a while, you can think more clearly about a problem."

"I walked away from it today, and that didn't do much good!" George pointed out.

Loudly.

"Excuse me!" said Mrs. Hertz. Her sharp, owlish eyes scanned the room from behind thick horn-rimmed eyeglasses. "Who's talking back there?"

Without looking away from the window, Patricia Volt pointed a finger at George.

"So much for feeling sorry for *her*," George grumbled to himself.

"Okay, Mr. Gearing," said Mrs. Hertz, crossing her arms. "What is so important that you need to interrupt my class to discuss it?"

"Nothing, Mrs. Hertz," George murmured.

"Did your alleged illness make you forget how to behave in school?"

20th century
- new technology improved communication and transport.
- mass production brought [...] biles and other high-tech goods to me[...] consumers

RADIO

"No, Mrs. Hertz."

"In that case, can you please remind me what I was talking about?"

"Something about the Industrial Revolution?" said George hopefully.

"Nice try, George," replied Mrs. Hertz. "But you'll need to do better than that to pass next week's exam. I was saying that in the twentieth century there was a huge breakthrough in communications technology, which contributed enormously to the second industrial revolution. Does the name Marconi mean anything to any of you?"

"Radio!" Anne piped up. She still hadn't gotten over the initial excitement of being in school with other human beings.

"Quite right, Miss Droid," said Mrs. Hertz. "Marconi was an Italian scientist who discovered that radio waves could be used to transmit information in the form of sound . . ."

Radio waves, George thought. *Everyone knows that.*

Suddenly, an idea struck him with such force that it nearly knocked him out of his chair.

"That's it!" he exclaimed, jumping to his feet. "Radio waves!"

He was halfway through mentally designing a schematic before he realized that the whole class was staring at him.

"Poor kid," Patricia said, shaking her head. "Totally insane—and so young!"

Her gang laughed and rolled their eyes.

"George, explain yourself this instant!" Mrs. Hertz said.

"Oh, sorry," he replied, red creeping into his cheeks. "Just got a little overexcited about the lesson, I guess." He slid slowly back into his seat.

"What was that all about?" Anne whispered, once Mrs. Hertz had resumed her lecture.

"I'll fill you in later," George murmured.

George kept quiet for the rest of class, but his mind was buzzing. *Radio!* he thought. *That's how I can send the information from the central computer to the conversion chamber! It's an old trick, but I bet there's an old radio in Otto's junkyard I can disassemble . . . Maybe, just maybe, I'll get lucky.*

It felt like an eternity before the bell finally rang. George leaped up and began stuffing books in his backpack as fast as he could.

"So, what's the big discovery about radio?" Anne asked.

"Sorry, I can't talk about it now," said George. "I need to get to the lab!"

"But—"

"I'll call you later!"

Anne bit her lip. "Sure, George," she said. "Whatever you want."

"See you!" George said as he rocketed out of the classroom.

He dashed down the corridor and was approaching the front entrance when he slipped on the polished linoleum. George yelped, wind-milling his arms as he skidded across the floor. He would have fallen but someone grabbed him by the front of his shirt.

"Whoa there!" Mr. Cog said. The old school janitor stood over George, a mop and bucket by his side. "Slow down, kid! What's the big rush?"

"Oh, sorry—I just had a serious eureka moment!" said George.

Mr. Cog wagged a thick finger in George's face. "Well, eureka moment or not, if you don't slow down and watch where you're going, you're going to get hurt."

"Okay, sure, Mr. Cog," George said, and burst out of the door at top speed. *Today is the day I make it work,* he thought. *I can feel it.* Everything and everyone else could wait.

4

The junkyard was quiet—too quiet.

Since all the abandoned robots had arrived, Otto's yard had been hopping with activity. The bots worked from dawn until dusk making so many improvements that the place was virtually unrecognizable. But when George arrived at the yard after school, there didn't seem to be anything happening at all.

"Hello?" George called out, opening the gate. "Is anyone here?" He scanned the area and saw Jackbot sitting on a rusty metal barrel, looking glum. "Jackbot," George said, walking over to him. "What's going on? Where is everyone?"

"Oh, you know," Jackbot said. "Around."

"But where?" George asked, searching the yard. "I don't see—"

But then he did. There were robots all around him, sitting on piles of scrap metal, lying on the ground and resting against the fence. George had mistaken them for pieces of junk. "Why are all the robots sitting there like that?"

"They're bored," Jackbot answered. "They finished cleaning and organizing everything in the entire yard two days ago. There's nothing else for them to do now, so most of them powered down into sleep mode."

"Huh," George said, thoughtful. He spied HP hanging upside down from the arm of Otto's power magnet, like a bat. His screen head displayed nothing but static. "They look so . . . depressed."

Jackbot hopped off the barrel and kicked a rock across the yard. "Yes, well—it's no fun being useless. One day you're an essential part of your human's life"—he looked pointedly into George's eyes—"and the next day, you're nothing at all."

George was about to argue when a screech of tires announced the arrival of a long white limousine at the junkyard's gate. The personalized license plate read VOLTMOBILE.

The car door swung open and a tall, deeply tanned man got out. "That's Patricia's dad," George muttered. "What's *he* doing here?" Maximilian Volt was the head of marketing at TinkerTech, and like his daughter, wasn't George's biggest fan. George couldn't think of why the man would be at Otto's junkyard—until he saw what Mr. Volt lifted out of the car. A sleek silver robot, two feet tall, with blue LED eyes. George recognized it at once.

"Cookie . . ." George heard Jackbot whisper.

Mr. Volt marched over to the junkyard gate and unceremoniously dumped Cookie onto the curb. "Sayonara, robot," he said, brushing the dirt from his hands. "You've trimmed your last nose hair!" And without another word, he climbed back into his car and sped away.

George couldn't believe his eyes. Patricia's state-of-the-art meBot must have cost as much as George's entire house. Had things gotten so bad that Mr. Volt was willing to surrender his family's expensive bot, too?

After a moment, Cookie rose from the ground and hovered in the air. A pair of delicate metallic arms emerged from her silver body, and she began to dust herself off with a brush attachment.

"My dearest love is in trouble!" Jackbot announced, springing into action. George followed him to the front gate. Cookie had completed her self-cleaning and was gazing up and down the street.

"Cookie!" Jackbot said, opening his arms wide. "I have come to rescue you!"

The little meBot swiveled to face them. "Oh," she said. "It is you again. I am in no need of rescue. I must await the return of my humans."

"Sorry, but I don't think they're coming back," George said.

Cookie's eyes flashed as she tried to process this puzzling information. "Then why have I been left in this place?"

"Um . . ." George didn't know how to tell her.

Just then Otto crossed the yard, pushing a wheelbarrow filled with spare parts. When he saw Cookie, he stopped and stared. "Another one?" he complained. "These bots are going to drive me out of house and home. Do you have any idea how much space they take up? Look around!"

George saw Cookie's eyes taking in Otto's oil-spotted overalls, his shaggy beard, and his grime-encrusted fingernails. "I think I understand," she said. "I've been sent here to groom this messy, unsightly man!" There was a double click, and one of her hands transformed into a pair of scissors, the other into a fine-tooth comb. "Prepare yourself for upgrade. Maximum makeover protocol initiated," she said, advancing on Otto.

"Ah, no thanks," Otto said, backing away.

"I must insist," Cookie said, floating nearer.

Otto turned and ran, with Cookie in pursuit.

"Cookie! Come back!" said Jackbot, and took off after them with his arms outstretched.

Well, at least that will keep them busy for a while,

George thought, and he returned to his task. The cleanup had made it much easier to find things in the yard, and George soon located a stack of radios, all different sizes and models. He spotted a big old car radio that looked perfect for the job and yanked it out of the pile. He was carrying it across the yard when he heard the sound of electronic barking, and then saw Sparky bound in through the gate, followed by Anne.

"Hey," George said, surprised. "I didn't expect to see you here."

"Why not?" Anne asked. "Because you've been

treating me like the invisible woman for the past few weeks?"

George looked at the ground. "Pretty much . . . yeah."

Anne punched him in the shoulder playfully. "Well, you're going to have to try harder than that to get rid of me, you big nerd. The way you ran out of school today, I figured you had some sort of breakthrough with the machine," Anne said. "I wasn't going to miss out on seeing that—even if you didn't bother to tell me about it."

"Look," George said with a sigh. "I know I've been preoccupied lately. It's just—I'm so close to seeing my parents again."

Anne nodded, and a flash of sadness crossed her face. It suddenly struck George that Anne was suffering too. He remembered everything she had told him about her father. Professor Droid's entire career could be in ruins, and they both might have to leave town for good. What must it be like for Anne to walk down the street? Did people stare? Did the other kids in school say mean things to her? George had been so caught up in his own problems, he hadn't even thought to ask.

"About your dad," he said, feeling awkward. "People in town are acting like idiots, turning their backs on the man who put this place on the map. They'll come around in the end, I'm sure of it."

"That makes one of us," Anne said grimly. "But thanks for saying it, anyway." She smiled at him, and George felt his heart lift.

"So," he said, scuffing the ground with his shoe. "Want to see what I've been doing?"

Anne grinned, her blue eyes sparkling. "I thought you'd never ask!" They raced down to the lab, with Sparky at their heels. "So what does Marconi have to do with all of this?"

"You see this radio?" George said, hefting it in his arms. "It's the last piece of the puzzle. When I hook this up to the central computer, Project Mercury should —fingers crossed—finally work!" At the bottom of the metal staircase, Anne got her first glimpse of the rebuilt

Project Mercury device. It looked nearly as impressive as it had before the explosion. There was quite a bit of duct tape, and the electro-oscillator was made out of soda cans . . . but everything was in place.

"You've really outdone yourself this time, Robot Boy," Anne said, shaking her head in disbelief.

George got busy dismantling the car radio and installing the correct components into the central computer. "If I tune it to the right frequency," he said as he worked, "I'll be able to transmit the information wirelessly to the conversion chamber." He stuck his arm into the rat's nest of wires inside the computer and pulled

out a handful. "The chamber should translate the radio waves into matter, and then . . ." George realized his hands were shaking.

"Don't worry, George," Anne said softly. "If it doesn't work this time, you'll just keep trying, right?"

George couldn't bear the thought of failure. "It *has* to work," he said. "It has to." He pulled the marble from his pocket, turned to the central computer, and placed the marble in the little silver hollow at the top of the machine.

There was a deep, low hum as Project Mercury came to life. The rebuilt components began clicking and vibrating and beeping and flashing with a rainbow of lights. George stood, staring at the Ready light, waiting for it to illuminate. Moments later, it glowed like a tiny sun.

"Here we go!" he said. "Ready?"

"Ready!" Anne replied.

With one trembling finger, he pushed the activation button.

The humming got louder and louder, until the whole

room was shaking from the vibration of the machine. Tools clattered to the ground, and George had to hold on to the console to keep his balance. A white light was bursting from the edges of the conversion chamber, getting brighter until it was almost blinding.

"It's happening!" George shouted. Any moment now, his parents would materialize right in front of his eyes!

But then the humming stuttered and the white light dimmed. Red warning lights began to flash on the computer console, and George scanned the data filling up the display screen, his heart in his throat. Desperately, he tapped at the controls, trying to bypass the errors, but only seconds after he was certain that he'd soon be in his parents' arms, the entire machine groaned like a man in pain and sputtered to a stop.

Silence filled the lab.

George felt his knees buckle beneath him, and sat down heavily on a metal work stool.

"George . . . ?" Anne's voice seemed to come from far away. "Are you okay?"

Disappointment crashed over him. He felt like he

had rolled an enormous boulder up a mountain, only to watch it tumble all the way down to the bottom again. What had gone wrong? One of the components had failed at the critical moment—but which one? He'd probably have to take the whole thing apart to figure it out.

"It's all right," Anne murmured, and George felt her hand on his shoulder. "You'll find a way to fix it—you always do!"

"Not this time," George said. "I think you should leave, Anne. I—I'd like to be alone now."

"But George—" she protested.

"*Please!*" George barked, his voice breaking. "Please. Just . . . go."

He felt Anne's hand leave his shoulder. "All right," she said quietly. "We'll go. Come on, Sparky."

It wasn't until Anne's footsteps had faded to silence that he allowed himself to cry.

After a few minutes, George dashed the tears from his eyes and took a deep breath. He spent ten minutes exhausting every option in his mind, every possible choice he could make—but no matter where his ideas led, they always came back to the same awful choice. *There's no other way,* he thought to himself. George slouched back in his seat, the weight of his decision heavy on his shoulders.

He was glad Anne was gone. She wouldn't approve of what he was about to do.

Pulling his old tablet from his backpack, George opened a command prompt and typed in the IP address he'd seen on the Caretaker's display screen. He told the computer to ping the address, and waited.

A moment later, a new page opened up. WELCOME, GEORGE GEARING, it said at the top.

George tapped the message field and typed: IT'S A DEAL, MICRON. TONIGHT I BREAK YOU OUT OF PRISON. TOMORROW I WANT MY PARENTS BACK.

Almost immediately, the reply appeared: A WISE CHOICE, GEARING. CARETAKER WILL CALL AT MIDNIGHT. DON'T BE LATE!

5

A soft, tinny melody woke George from uneasy dreams.

Jackbot was sitting at the end of George's bed, his eyes glowing green in the darkness. "It's time," he said. He touched a button on the side of his head and the music stopped.

George threw the blankets off and sat up. He shivered—but not from the cold.

"Are you sure you want to do this?" Jackbot asked. He'd been posing that same question since George had told him about the plan when they got home from the junkyard.

"I've told you a million times, JB," George whispered. "It's the only way. Now are you with me or not?"

"I'm with you," Jackbot muttered. "But I want you to know that this plan is capricious, harebrained, and intolerably reckless."

"If it gets my parents back, I don't care how crazy it is," George said, groping for his glasses and putting them on. "Okay, let's get moving."

He slipped into the clothes he'd laid out—black jeans, black shirt, black sneakers, and a black woolen cap. Squinting at the mirror, he dabbed black face paint on his cheeks, forehead, and nose, then picked up a can of spray paint and turned to his robot friend. "Okay, Jackbot. Hold still—we don't want anyone recognizing you!" He sprayed the black paint over the shiny parts of Jackbot's body. "Oh, don't worry—it'll wash off with a little soap and water." Soon Jackbot was an almost invisible shadow, except for his gleaming eyes.

George stood back to examine his work. "All right then. Are you ready?" he asked.

"I guess so," said Jackbot.

George snatched up a small black backpack and pulled open the zipper to check that his secret weapon was still inside. The moonlight caught on the tiny, silvery bodies of the objects within. Satisfied, George pulled the zipper shut and slung the backpack over his shoulder. He and Jackbot tiptoed across the landing and downstairs. The sound of snoring, loud as a buzz saw, came from Otto's room.

A cold wind met them as they stepped out into the backyard. It was a cloudy night, crowned with a sliver of crescent moon and a few scattered stars.

"The Caretaker should be here any minute," George said. "What's the time?"

"Twenty-three hours, fifty-eight minutes, and sixteen seconds," Jackbot replied. He grabbed George's shirt with his metal claw. "George, wait! Don't you remember what your father said when he and your mom appeared above the marble? They told you not to trust Micron, 'under any circumstances.' Why in the world do you think you can trust him now?"

"Of course I remember," said George. In fact, he had been replaying his father's words in his head since the moment he had agreed to help Micron escape. "But

I have a plan—just in case Micron tries to double-cross us."

"Really?" Jackbot asked. "What is it?"

But before George could answer, he heard what sounded like leaves and twigs crackling under heavy tires. Something was coming.

Out of the gloom, two yellow eyes appeared. "It is midnight, George Gearing," said the Caretaker. "Are you prepared to commence with the mission?"

George looked at Jackbot and gave him a reassuring wink. "Sure," George said. "But before we go, can you settle something for us? I think that star to the left of the moon is Arcturus, but Jackbot says it's Betelgeuse. Which is it?"

The Caretaker swiveled around, tilted its head upward, and stared at the sky. Without hesitation, George leaped on the huge robot's back and reached for a tiny, hidden panel at the base of its neck. George quickly opened the panel and exposed a numerical keypad. Nervously, he tapped in a six-digit code and waited.

Click.

The Caretaker instantly powered down, its head lolling and its arms dropping to its sides. After everything he and the behemoth had gone through, George was surprised to find how easy it was to shut it down.

"Sweet dreams!" said George, climbing off its back. He cocked his head in thought. "Not that robots dream . . . do they?"

"I do," Jackbot answered. "About Cookie, mostly."

"Well, that figures. I wonder what this brute would dream about."

"Killing people, probably," Jackbot replied. "How'd you manage to turn him off? That would have been nice to know one of those times he was trying to kill us."

George chuckled. "It was OCD-Bot that gave me the idea. Even though the programming was different, I was hoping the designs for both robots' security measures were the same. I found OCD-Bot's schematics on the Tinker Tech servers and found the panel. Looks like they didn't bother changing Micron's original security code when they built OCD-Bot. It's his birthday."

Jackbot shook his head in wonder. "You're so clever, it's almost criminal," he said. "Why did you deactivate him, though? I thought he was going to take us to Micron?"

"You'll see," George said. "Can you open up his chest panel?"

Jackbot opened the little door in his midriff and pulled out an electronic screwdriver. He speedily removed the cover from the Caretaker's panel. George reached inside and accessed the robot's central processing unit. "Working on Project Mercury has taught me a few new tricks, you big hunk of junk," he whispered to the unconscious Caretaker.

A few minutes later, he was done with the chest panel and Jackbot had screwed the cover back into place. The robot stirred, its eyes flashing red as it rebooted.

"No star-mapping program available," it said, picking up right where it had left off.

"Forget it," said George. "We have more important things to worry about tonight than the stars. Let's go!"

. . .

George and Jackbot clung to the Caretaker's back as the robot flew through the night, propelled by its powerful thrusters. The cold wind ruffled George's hair and numbed his hands. Far below, George saw the twinkling lights of Terabyte Heights, clustered like a galaxy around the gleaming tower of TinkerTech HQ. The lights grew fewer as they reached the outskirts of town, then all but disappeared. Now they were above fields and forests so dark, it felt like soaring over a black hole. Then a blazing light loomed before them. A white monolith rose upward, with edges so sharp they looked like they could cut the sky itself.

Firewall Prison.

The roar from the Caretaker's thrusters dropped by several decibels, and they began to descend. A few moments later, they landed softly in the woods next to the prison.

George slid off the Caretaker's back and pushed through the shrubbery until he could get a good look at the entrance. Standing at attention in front of a twenty-foot-tall metal gate were two armed guards.

George hurried back to where he had left Jackbot and the Caretaker. "I thought I had planned for every possible obstacle," he whispered miserably, and slapped his head. "Except how to get past the front gate. How could I forget that?"

"No matter," said the Caretaker. "I will dispatch the guards with my circular saw!"

"No!" George exclaimed, a little too loudly, then

lowered his voice. "We have to do this without hurting anyone."

"I have an idea," Jackbot piped up. "A scheme, a strategy, a cunning plan. Wait here." And before George could stop him, he had trotted off through the trees.

George and the Caretaker waited. It was silent in the woods except for the chirp of crickets and the low voices on the guards' ancient radio that was playing oldies from the early twenty-first century.

"We are exactly twelve minutes behind schedule," said the Caretaker. "Please locate your automated trash can immediately."

"He's not a trash can!" George said. "And I know we're running late! I'm sure he'll show up soon . . ."

I hope . . . he thought.

Just then George saw Jackbot walk into the clearing at the prison entrance, holding a large, steaming pizza box. *"Jackbot!"* George hissed. *"What are you doing?!"* But if the robot heard him, he didn't show it. Jackbot approached the guards, who looked at him in surprise, one slinging the gun off his shoulder.

"State your business!" demanded the tall burly guard who quickly readied his gun.

"Pizza-delivery," droned Jackbot in the flat, monotonous voice of a basic service-bot.

"Pizza? For who?"

"For-you," said Jackbot.

"What? We didn't order a pizza."

"I-can-confirm-a-pizza-was-ordered," Jackbot continued in a monotone.

The second guard eyed Jackbot with suspicion. "I thought everyone stopped using robots . . ."

"Luigi-was-sick-today," Jackbot intoned. "I-am-just-filling-in."

The two guards exchanged a glance.

"You think the boss ordered it for us?" said one.

The other shrugged. "Who cares? It's hot, and I'm starving."

"Yeah—no point looking a gift horse in the mouth, am I right?"

"It-is-not-a-horse," said Jackbot. "It-is-a-pizza."

The guards grinned. "Okay, little guy—we'll take it."

Jackbot handed the pizza over and then trotted back through the trees, where he joined George and the Caretaker on the other side.

"What was that all about?" George asked.

"Wait-and-see," said Jackbot. "I mean, wait and see!"

The guards had torn off large slices of pizza and were gobbling them down like they hadn't eaten for a week. Halfway through the second slice, one of them began fanning his brow. George watched as the other guard's face turned pink, then red, then an unhealthy shade of purple.

"Yeow!" that one said, panting. "This pizza is . . . really . . . spicy!"

"You're telling me!" said the other, his face shiny with sweat. "My mouth is on fire!"

The two guards looked at each other, their eyes bulging, and yelled, "WATER!"

They dropped the pizza, dragged opened the gate, and ran inside, clutching their throats.

When the sounds of the guards' footsteps had receded, George, Jackbot, and the Caretaker walked back through the trees into the clearing that faced the prison. "Okay, I'm impressed," George said to Jackbot. "How'd you do it?"

"It was easy," Jackbot replied. "I simply called in an order to the nearest pizzeria, pretending to be a guard, and told them to deliver it to the prison gate. The kid who delivered it seemed a little surprised to see a robot waiting there, but I put a few extra bucks in his hand and he forgot all about his worries. As far as my special toppings, I always keep a few of these"—he held up a round orange pepper—"in my chest compartment. Habanero peppers—about 200,000 on the Scoville heat scale. Not hot enough to kill you, but hot enough to make you stop caring about guard duty."

George stared at him, amazed.

"What?" Jackbot asked. "I only hurt them a little bit. Besides, they're the ones who took food from a stranger. Serves them right."

"No, it's not that," George said. "You're, well—anyway, what else do you keep in that chest compartment of yours?"

"This and that," Jackbot replied, opening the door in his chest. George saw a ball of string, a bottle labeled "Invisible Ink," a pair of 3D glasses, a fake mustache, a water pistol, and a jumble of other miscellaneous objects.

"Wow, Jackbot!" George exclaimed. "Have you got everything in the world in there or what?"

"No, George," Jackbot answered, as if he were talking to a baby. "That wouldn't be possible."

George rolled his eyes. "C'mon, you two—before the guards come back!"

The three of them raced through the empty, unguarded gate and into the prison entrance hall. The Caretaker kept himself a few steps ahead of George, his

red eyes scanning the area. It was a lofty, echoing space with corridors in every direction, and security cameras mounted on each wall.

"Okay, *this* I planned for!" George said. "Jackbot, lend me your screwdriver—and give me a boost."

George clambered onto the robot's shoulders until he was level with the nearest security camera. Working quickly, George opened the back of one and located a small console with a keyboard and a tiny monitor. *Nothing too complicated here,* he thought. Bypassing the camera's basic security protocols, George typed the command "Default for All Cameras" into the settings to enable the playback option on every unit.

"Done!" he said, jumping to the ground. "Every camera in the whole place will now show empty corridors on a thirty-second loop—we'll be invisible wherever we go!"

"Smart work, George," Jackbot said, adding, "For a human."

"What is that supposed to mean?" demanded George.

"Joke, George. Remember those?"

"You know, there are times when I regret upgrading your sense-of-humor software," George said, trying not to smile. "Okay, buddy, where do we go from here?"

Before they had left home, Jackbot had downloaded a floor plan of the prison. His eyes flashed as he accessed it. "Central corridor. We follow it to the elevator, which leads to Block H on the top floor," he said. "That's where they keep all the cyber criminal masterminds."

"*All* of them? You mean there's more than one?"

Jackbot shrugged. "It's a surprisingly lucrative career choice, apparently. Unless you get caught—which they usually do. For being so diabolically brilliant, those supervillains are actually pretty dopey."

"Well, it's one of those dopes' lucky day," said George. "But before we go, there's something I need to do . . ."

He dug into his backpack and pulled out a handful of silver moth-bots. His secret weapon.

"Yow!" said Jackbot, hiding behind the Caretaker.

"Are you crazy? Demented? Deranged? Those moth-bots are deadly!"

George chuckled. "Not these. I found them when I was working in my parents' lab. Micron must have been using them to collect intel, but they survived the explosion. I thought they might come in handy, so I reprogrammed them to work for me. These little guys will report back if they sense any guards approaching."

He tossed the tiny spies into the air, and they flew off in different directions.

George, Jackbot, and the Caretaker followed the central corridor, but soon came to a pair of locked steel doors.

"Caretaker!" said George. "Do your stuff!"

"Shall I use the blowtorch or the sledgehammer?" it asked.

"Neither!" George exclaimed. "Is your default setting 'psychopath' or what? Use your *key attachment!*"

"Your method is dull but acceptable." The Caretaker scanned the lock, and a few seconds later its arm retracted, then reappeared topped with a spiky bunch of keys. There was a series of clicks as the arm rotated them, trying to find a match. After a few seconds, it made a selection and inserted the key, and the door swung open soundlessly.

They went through and George closed the door behind them, so that if a guard passed by he wouldn't see it ajar.

They reached the elevator without being spotted. Beside it was a glass panel. A small sign next to the panel read AUTHORIZED PERSONNEL ONLY. ALIGN EYE WITH GLASS FOR RETINAL SCAN.

George's breath caught in his throat. "Where is the control panel?" he said. "There's supposed to be a control panel!"

"Hmm," Jackbot said, inspecting the scanner. "It looks like this equipment has been recently upgraded."

"But I can't break into the elevator without being able to access the controls!" George said, trying not to panic. "What are we going to do now?"

"Maybe there's another way to disable the controls?" wondered Jackbot.

"Indeed," said the Caretaker. It raised its arm, which swiveled into a sledgehammer attachment, and swung it toward the glass panel.

"Wait!" George shouted.

The Caretaker's sledgehammer stopped an inch from the glass. "Your reluctance to smash things is highly inconvenient, George Gearing," the robot said.

"If we destroy the controls, we'll set off every alarm in the place!" George said. "We have to be more subtle."

"But how?" Jackbot asked.

Suddenly, a silver moth-bot came whizzing down the corridor toward them.

"Oh, no," said George. "A guard must be coming!"

"Quick, George, think of something!" said Jackbot.

"Why don't *you* think of something?"

"I can't!"

"Well, neither can I!"

"Shall I smash it, then?" asked the Caretaker.

"No!" said George and Jackbot in unison.

The next moment, a guard came walking around the corner. He was tall and skinny with a straggly mustache and the name OFFICER BOOLEAN stitched onto the breast pocket of his jacket. He was walking with a little spring in his step, singing softly to himself.

His eyes went wide at the sight of George and the robots, and the words of the song died in his throat.

"Don't move!" he shouted. "Who are you? What are you doing here?"

6

"Um, hi," George said to the guard, who was fumbling for his gun. "Look, I can explain—"

"Explanations are unnecessary," the Caretaker droned, advancing on the man. Boolean managed to pull his gun out of its holster, but before he could so much as point it at them, the Caretaker had grabbed it from him and crushed it like tissue paper. Boolean goggled at his ruined weapon, speechless. "Your existence is detrimental to our mission," the Caretaker continued. "Stand by to be terminated."

Boolean paled and groped for the walkie-talkie at his belt, but it was too late. The Caretaker struck at the guard's neck with a claw, collapsing him in a motionless heap.

George gasped. "Caretaker! I told you not to hurt anyone!" he shouted.

"The human is merely unconscious," the robot replied. "Robots are not the only ones with Off buttons."

"Oh," George said, relieved. "What was all that 'stand by for termination' stuff then, if you were just knocking him out?"

The massive robot raised its arms as if in a shrug. "Old programming dies hard."

"On the bright side," Jackbot said, "looks like we've got ourselves an authorized set of retinas!"

"Right," said George, glancing down at Officer Boolean. He was out cold. "Let's do this quickly!"

The Caretaker hoisted the unconscious guard to a sitting position and pressed his face against the glass panel. George pried open one of Boolean's eyes, and a moment later the elevator door pinged open.

While Jackbot held down a button inside the elevator to keep the door open, George swiped the walkie-talkie from the guard's belt, in case anyone tried to contact him. "Now let's hide him inside that supply closet," George said, gesturing to a small door right next to the elevator. "Gently."

The Caretaker swiftly opened the closet door and tossed the guard inside like a sack of potatoes. As he landed, there was a crash of mops and cleaning supplies. "I said *gently!*" George objected.

"I am the Caretaker," the robot said. "For me, that *was* gentle."

George shook his head and motioned the Caretaker into the elevator.

Once they were all inside, George pressed the button

for the top floor. The doors swished shut and the elevator began to rise, swiftly and silently.

When the elevator had reached its destination, the doors opened to reveal yet another door—heavy, windowless, and equipped with five different locks.

"Keys, Caretaker," George said. "This one is going to be tricky." While the robot was busy selecting the right keys, Boolean's walkie-talkie crackled. George jumped, as if a grenade had gone off in his hand.

"Hey, Boolean," said a voice. "Everything all right up there? Over."

George looked at Jackbot. "What do I do?" he mouthed.

Jackbot took the walkie-talkie from him and pressed the speak button. "Everything is fine and dandy, my friend," he said, in a perfect imitation of Boolean's voice. "Peachy keen. Absolutely nothing to worry about in the least. One hundred percent A-OK. Over."

There was a pause, and George's heart pounded in his chest. Then there was laughter on the other end. "I think you've been on one too many graveyard shifts,

Boolean!" the guard chortled. "Well, there's only six hours to go—so try not to go all weird on me before your shift ends. Over and out!"

George let out a breath he hadn't realized he was holding. "That was close," he said. "How did you manage to imitate his voice, JB? He barely said one sentence before he was out cold!"

"One sentence was sufficient to identify timbre, intonation, and characteristic vowel sounds," said Jackbot.

The Caretaker had unbolted four of the locks and was working on the fifth. Then there was one more loud click and the steel door swung open. Motioning for Jackbot and the Caretaker to stay behind and be on the lookout for more guards, George proceeded alone through the doorway. Behind it was a short hallway, ending in a floor-to-ceiling glass door. Behind that was a man reclining in a wooden chair, flipping casually through a computer magazine. He made even the orange prison jumpsuit he wore look good.

Micron.

George reached for the mechanized door handle

and gave it two quick turns to the left and one to the right, like he'd read in the downloaded schematics. At the sound of the door opening, Micron looked up and smiled. "Ah, Mr. Gearing," he said. "Right on time."

The sight of Micron brought home the reality of what George was doing. *This guy is evil!* George's brain cried out. *How many times has he tried to kill you? Three? Four?* George put his hand in his pocket and wrapped his fingers around the marble. *Focus on Mom and Dad,* he told himself, silencing his doubts. *You're doing this for them.*

"Let's go, Micron," George said, his voice stern. "I've kept my word. Now it's your turn."

Micron rose to his feet and sauntered over. "Of course I will," he said, reaching out to shake George's hand. "A deal is a deal."

A chill ran down George's back. The last time Micron had shaken George's hand was when they had first met, down in the TinkerTech robotics lab. Micron had been a hero to him then. "One thing I don't understand," George said as they walked out of the cell and down the hallway. "Why me? The Caretaker could have busted you out of this place weeks ago."

"The Caretaker has many virtues," Dr. Micron answered. "But as you know, subtlety isn't one of them. He'd have smashed his way in and taken out half the guards doing it, but they'd have eventually stopped him, and a lot of good and decent people would have died in the process. And my imprisonment has taught me to be a more merciful man—and a smarter one as well. No, the job required someone with real brains. Naturally, I thought of you." They had reached the other side of the steel door, where Jackbot and the Caretaker were waiting.

George hated himself for blushing, but despite his bloodthirsty nature, Dr. Micron was still one of the most brilliant minds on the planet—and there he was, praising George's intelligence. It was hard not to feel flattered.

"You were the only one who could pull it off, George," Micron continued. "We may have had our differences in the past, but there's no denying that you're the smartest young man I've ever met."

"Thanks," George said, shuffling his feet.

"Sorry to interrupt this love-in," Jackbot cut in. "But last time I checked, this is a prison break, not couples therapy. So can we please get on with it, before we have to join him back in that cell?"

Freed from the spell of Micron's charm, George nodded. "Jackbot's right," he said, turning back to Micron. "You said you'd help me get my parents back. How is that going to work?"

"I want to be perfectly honest with you, George," Micron said, sincerity shining from his handsome, chiseled face. "Being stuck in that cell has given me a lot of time to think, and I've seen the error of my ways. It pains me to know how many people I've hurt in my quest for power, and I want to do something about it. Starting with you. Helping you bring your mom and dad back is my first step on the road to redemption. After we fix that machine, I'll make a fresh start. New name, new town—I'll leave Terabyte Heights for good. Get me out of here and you won't just be saving your parents' lives, you'll be saving mine."

George looked at Micron, trying to find something to distrust in his eyes. But all George could see was his own frightened face, reflected back at him. "Fine," George said. "But we have to hurry. It's only a matter of time before they notice—"

AWOOGA! AWOOGA!

An earsplitting alarm sounded and red lights flashed down every hallway. George staggered and clasped his hands to the sides of his head.

An urgent, amplified voice echoed through the prison: "INTRUDER ALERT. INTRUDER ALERT. ALL ARMED PERSONNEL REPORT TO SECTION H IMMEDIATELY!"

"I think they noticed," said Jackbot.

George broke into a sweat. "We can't get out the way we came—the whole place is on lockdown!"

"I suspected this might happen," Dr. Micron said calmly. "That's where you come in, Caretaker. I had hoped to avoid wanton destruction, but alas, wanton destruction it must be. Climb aboard, everyone!" He stood on one of the Caretaker's wheel guards to get up behind the robot's broad back, and George and Jackbot clambered onto the other side.

"Get us out of here!" Dr. Micron shouted.

"Yes, quickly, Caretaker!" George added. "The guards are coming!"

The mighty robot's engines began to rumble. As the Caretaker raised its steel arms above its head, the two pincers swiveled into demolition balls. A moment later the Caretaker rocketed straight up, so abruptly that George felt like he'd left his stomach behind. He was still gasping at the suddenness of it all when the Caretaker's massive metal arms smashed through the prison ceiling.

The next instant they were blasted by cold air as they sailed up into the sky. Glancing down, George saw a jagged hole in the roof of the prison, white light shining through it like a hole in the night. The wail of the sirens faded as the Caretaker leveled out and began to fly back toward Terabyte Heights.

"I can't believe it," George breathed. "We did it."

Micron clapped him on the back with one hand. "Of course we did," he said. "Didn't I tell you we'd make a great team? Now, I'd like a shower and a fresh change of clothes. Orange does *nothing* for me. We can reconvene in the morning and get started on Project Mercury. Ah, I see my house over there on the right. Caretaker—fly me home!"

But the Caretaker flew right over Micron's house.

"Hey!" Micron objected. "What's wrong with you? Didn't I just upgrade your systems to MANIA-CAL 3.0?"

"Oh, I forgot to mention," George said casually. "I did a little reprogramming on the Caretaker. He obeys *my* orders now. And I'm not letting you out of my sight until you've fulfilled your part of the deal."

Dr. Micron's face darkened like a thundercloud for an instant, but then the clouds parted and he was all sunny smiles again. "I said you were smart, George, and I'm always right. Fine. It's your game now. Where to, boss?"

"Caretaker," George commanded. "Take us to my place!"

Half an hour later, George was peeking out of
his bedroom window, checking that the Caretaker was
still standing at its station by the front hedges. He
already knew that Jackbot was watching the back door.
With the two robots on guard duty, George might actually get some sleep tonight. It was no use going straight
to the junkyard. The place was locked up tight, and he
didn't want to attract any unwanted attention. They'd
have to wait until the next morning and accompany
Otto to the yard as usual.

George turned back to the room and caught Micron
picking a bunch of discarded items out of the trash basket next to the desk—articles about Micron and photos

of him that used to decorate George's wall. "You should really hang on to these," Micron said, holding up a photograph of himself from the cover of *TechWeek* magazine, which had named him Genius of the Year. "They might be worth something one day."

George marched over, snatched the papers and photos out of Micron's hands, and dumped them back into the trash. "I doubt it," he replied.

Micron shrugged. Next to the trash basket was the sleeping bag George had given him, and he leaned over to pick it up. "Well, it's your loss," he said, unrolling the bag and climbing in. Snuggling down inside the covers, he yawned. "Face it, George," he said, closing his eyes. "You and I are more alike than you want to admit."

"I'm nothing like you," George said. "You're a criminal!"

"Says the kid who just broke into Firewall Prison." Micron chuckled and closed his eyes. "You should be thrilled to be like me, George. After all, isn't that what you've always wanted?"

George said nothing, and a few moments later he heard Micron's breathing become slow and rhythmic.

George lay awake in bed, staring at the shadows the streetlights cast on his ceiling. *If he's the guilty one,* George thought, *why am I the one who can't sleep?*

"You want *another* day off from school?" Otto said, slamming the truck door shut. "I told you already, George—enough is enough!"

"One more day," George pleaded. "I promise. Just one and I won't ask again. Please?"

"I'm running out of excuses to tell your teacher," Otto grumbled.

"Say I got food poisoning," George said. "Say I ate a bad egg!"

"You *are* a bad egg."

Jackbot hooted from the back seat. "Oh, I love it when you utilize metaphor to create humor, Otto! Have you ever considered a second career as a comedian?"

Otto puffed up his chest a little, like a rooster. "Well, I

did do some improv back in automotive school. Mostly car humor, though." He softened. "All right, George, you can take today off—but this is the last time, do you hear me?"

"Loud and clear," George said, grinning at Jackbot.

As Otto gunned the engine, George stole a glance at the back of the truck, where a grease-spattered tarp concealed two lumps: a huge square one and a smaller man-sized one. George and Jackbot had risen at the crack of dawn to hide Micron and the Caretaker in the truck before Otto woke up. If they could get to the junkyard without Otto suspecting anything, they'd be home free.

As they were driving along, George's back pocket vibrated, and he pulled out his battered old flip phone to find fifteen text messages and eight voicemails from

Anne. WHY AREN'T YOU ANSWERING YOUR PHONE? the messages read. ARE YOU OKAY? George flipped the phone closed again. It was safer not to bring Anne into this. She'd had enough to deal with, and anyway, she wouldn't understand.

"What in tarnation's going on here?" Otto exclaimed.

They were drawing up to the junkyard now, and could see a crowd of protesters surrounding the gate. There were many of the same faces they'd seen outside TinkerTech, and quite a few of the same signs. The red-headed woman with glasses was there, with a new sign. It said: HUMANS VS ROBOTS — WHOSE SIDE ARE YOU ON? She rushed up to the truck as soon as it pulled to a stop.

"This man is hoarding robots!" she shouted to the crowd. "He's even got one in this truck!"

Two, actually, George thought.

"So what's your plan?" she sneered, turning to Otto. "Are you building a robot army to take over Terabyte Heights? Are you one of those copycat criminals, trying to steal a little of Micron's limelight?"

"Of course not!" Otto spluttered. "Now get off my property before I call the police!"

The woman put her hands on her hips. "Not until you surrender those robots. They must be destroyed before something else catastrophic happens!"

Otto lifted his robotic arm so that the woman and the rest of the crowd could see it. "Then I guess you'll have to destroy me too," he growled. "Now move!"

The sight of Otto's arm momentarily stunned the woman, and she backed off. Otto took the opportunity to inch the truck forward, forcing the crowd to retreat. "George, take the key and open the gate—fast!"

It was scary, pushing his way through the hostile crowd, but George made it to the gate, inserted the key, and yanked the gate open. Otto hit the gas and George barely managed to slam and lock the gate behind him before the protestors could barrel inside the yard after them. He ran after the truck, which pulled in behind the junkyard's small office building, out of sight of the disgruntled mob.

Otto hopped down from the cab, wiped his brow

with the back of his beefy hand, and walked to the back of the truck. He puffed out his cheeks. "Good work, George. I've never seen people around here act so crazy before!"

"They are scared," Jackbot said. "Apprehensive, frightened, nervous. Humans often behave irrationally when they're afraid."

"Thanks for the psychology lesson, Professor," Otto said. "But there's no excuse for that kind of nastiness." He snorted. "Imagine them thinking I was trying to be like Micron!"

"Yes," George mumbled, feeling sick. "Imagine that."

"Like I'd ever want to be anything like that no-good piece of dirt," said Otto, leaning against the back of the truck where Micron lay hidden. "What a pathetic excuse for a human being that guy is! I wish he was here right now. I'd teach *him* a lesson he wouldn't forget!"

George gulped.

"The man is scum, you hear me? Something you wipe from your shoes! I hope he rots in jail for the rest of his miserable life."

"Boy, it's getting late, isn't it?" George piped up, glancing at his watch. He had to get Otto away before Micron burst out from under the tarp to throttle him. "Lots to do today!"

"Right," Otto said, snapping out of his tirade. "I'll be in my office, out of sight of those goons. Never thought I'd say this, but you'd best do the same, George. You'll be safer down in that lab."

George nodded, and Otto stumped off. Once his uncle was safely around the corner, George pulled down the back door of the truck. As he peeled back the tarp, Micron's disheveled, angry head popped up. "So, I'm something you wipe from your shoes now, am I?"

"Can you blame him?" George asked. "Besides, if you fix Project Mercury and bring back my parents, I'm sure Otto will change his mind. Now hurry—before anyone sees us!"

George did a quick scan of the area, then led Micron and the Caretaker over to the hatch with Jackbot bringing up the rear. "Well," said George, as he opened the hatch and motioned Dr. Micron down the steps. "Here we are again."

"As friends this time, not enemies—yes?" Micron said.

"Right," George replied. It was tempting to believe him—maybe he really had changed?

A few minutes later, Micron was standing in the center of the blackened lab, staring critically at all the homemade bits of equipment George had been working on for weeks. George watched him intently, surprised at how much he cared about what his former hero would say.

Micron narrowed his eyes at the soda cans and car batteries. When he finally looked back at George, he was smiling. "This is truly impressive. You have a real knack for innovation—all of these parts alone are merely garbage, but together . . . together they just might work. I see you've inherited your parents' ingenuity!"

George couldn't help it—he grinned. After so many years of feeling like a second-rate kid from a broken family, it was wonderful to be praised, and to hear his parents praised too—even if the compliments were coming from a villain.

"Now," Micron continued, "show me what happens when you try to run it."

As he'd done before, George began by warming up the machine. All the various components started humming, clicking, and flashing. George pushed the activation button. But right as the conversion was about to begin, all the pieces sputtered to a halt again.

"See?" George said. "Something is wrong, but I have no idea what it is."

"Hmm," Micron said, stroking his chin. "It's nearly there, that's for certain. Something is misfiring. I'm going to run a basic diagnostic check and see what I can find. Okay?"

Micron had started typing commands on the central computer console when George saw a familiar silver shape float down into the lab.

"Cookie!" Jackbot said, tripping over a chair and two trash cans to get to her. "What brings you to our humble lab?"

"All the other robots are asleep," Cookie complained. "And that filthy man Otto has locked himself inside his office, so I can't give him another pedicure. I am in search of activity."

"Well, then—it's your lucky day!" Jackbot exclaimed. "Activity is my middle name. Well, no—it's actually Captain Awesome, but that's a story for another time." The robot turned to the Caretaker, who was lurking in the corner of the lab. "Hey, blockhead," Jackbot said. "Meet Cookie. She's my girlfriend."

"I am not his girlfriend," Cookie said tonelessly.

This didn't seem to faze Jackbot. He turned to her with adoration in his LED eyes. "Isn't she charming?"

The Caretaker's big metal head swiveled to look at Cookie, and his photoelectric pupils dilated. "Greetings, Cookie. I am gratified to see you are equipped with the latest programming software. If you have enemies in need of annihilation, I am capable of fifty-seven different types of destruction. These include but are not limited to pulverization, incineration, and disembowelment—"

"Stop showing off," Jackbot snapped. "Forget about that goon, Cookie—you're too smart for the likes of him. Now," he said—whipping a black-and-white checkered board from his chest compartment—"how about a game of chess to pass the time?"

George raised an eyebrow. "You keep a *chess set* in there?"

"You never know when you'll need one," Jackbot replied. "So," he turned back to Cookie. "Think you're up to the challenge?"

"I can play chess at grand master level," Cookie said, haughtily. "I will wipe the floor with you."

"I can mop floors as well!" the Caretaker broke in, brandishing a mop attachment.

"It will take a lot more than a mop to win her over, Caretaker," Jackbot said as he set up the pieces. "Believe me, I know." He turned to Cookie. "There you are, my darling—it's your move."

After watching them play a few turns, George turned back to Dr. Micron. "Well?" he asked. "Any luck?"

"It's not the electro-oscillator," Micron said. "And

the recoding unit seems fully operational. Let's try the molecular analysis device . . ."

"George!" a voice called from above. "Are you down there?"

It was Anne! George heard her feet on the metal steps and whirled around to face Micron. "We've got to hide you—quick!" he whispered. He desperately scanned the room. "There! Get inside that broken fridge!"

Micron scoffed. "You must be joking."

"Nope, totally serious—now get in!" George shoved the man inside and slammed the door.

"Ugh, it smells like old cheese," Micron said, his voice muffled.

"Be quiet!" George waved the Caretaker away, too, and the big robot hid behind one of the conversion pods.

Anne reached the bottom of the steps with Sparky at her side. She caught sight of George standing in front of the fridge and trying to look casual.

"Oh, hi, Anne," he said. "How's it going?" Sparky scampered over to George and began sniffing curiously.

"That's all you have to say?" she sputtered. "'How's it going?' I've been trying to get in touch with you for days!"

"Yeah," George said, nudging Sparky away with his foot. "Sorry about that—my phone died and I've been too busy to charge it."

"Well, have you heard the news?" she asked breathlessly.

"What news?"

"Dr. Micron escaped from Firewall Prison!"

"Oh!" George said in a choked voice. "Oh—my gosh. That's . . . terrible!"

"Yeah! Some guys broke him out! On the news they said it was a short guy dressed all in black, a little black robot, and a big robot that sounded a lot like the Caretaker." She looked at George in disbelief. "How could you not have heard about this? It's all anyone has been talking about!"

"Well, I've been down here all day, so . . ."

Anne blinked, opening and closing her mouth like a fish out of water. "But . . . aren't you scared? I mean, it was because of you that he was arrested. He might come looking for revenge!"

"Nah," said George. "I'm not worried."

"Why not?" Anne exclaimed. "You are so completely obsessed with this Project Mercury thing, you can't even see what's right in front of your face! For all you know, Micron could be anywhere, waiting for the right moment to grab you!"

George swallowed hard. Micron chuckled.

"Did that refrigerator just laugh?" Anne asked.

George kicked the door behind him with the flat of his foot. "Of course not! It's a *fridge*, Anne. Now who's acting crazy?"

"Look," Anne said, angry now. "I don't know what's going on with you, George. I know you want your parents back, but you're pushing everyone else away to do it. I thought you were better than this."

"Well, I'm not," George said, eager for this

conversation to end. He didn't know how much air Micron had left inside the fridge. "So, I guess there's nothing else to say."

Anne shook her head, her eyes watery. "No, I guess there isn't." She turned around and ran back up the stairs. At first, Sparky seemed reluctant to leave the mystery of the smell unsolved, but finally he followed Anne, his claws clicking on the metal steps.

"You can come out now," George said numbly.

Micron toppled out, gasping. "Horrors!" he said, his eyes bulging. "I saw my life flashing before my eyes—and everything smelled like cheese."

"Ha!" said Jackbot, his suction cup on the black queen. He and Cookie had been so engrossed in their chess game that they had missed everything. "What do you think of that?"

Cookie's blue eyes studied the board. "It appears that we have reached a stalemate." She cocked her head at Jackbot, curious. "I do not comprehend your response to this result. Why are you pleased?"

"Because we both won. And what's better than that?"

"You would not have preferred to be the sole victor?"

"A victory is much sweeter if you have someone to share it with."

Cookie took a moment to process this. Then she said, "Shall we play again?"

George turned away from the two robots, trying to ignore the ugly, rotten feeling that had been building in his gut ever since Anne had stormed out. *If only she hadn't dropped in unannounced, I wouldn't have had to drive her away like that,* he reasoned. *But she's my best friend . . .*

George didn't have the chance to finish the thought, however—because in the next moment he felt Micron's heavy hand on his shoulder. "Good news, partner," he said with a toothy smile. "I think I've found your problem."

"You have?" George said, his heart soaring.
Micron led him back to the machine and pointed out a
component in the quantum particle accelerator.

"See this piece?" Micron said. "The mercury levels
are not nearly high enough. If this little guy isn't functioning at optimal level, the data won't transmute into
biomatter."

George wasn't completely surprised. This was the part
that had given him the most trouble. He had put together
a box with an electrical current that ran through a few
drops of mercury he'd removed from an old thermometer, which seemed a decent approximation to the original component. But apparently, it wasn't good enough.

"Fine, but can you fix it?" he asked anxiously.

Dr. Micron shook his head. "Sorry, George. We can't make it work with replacements. We need the real thing."

"Oh," George said, deflated.

"Don't lose heart yet, Gearing," Micron said, seeing the look on George's face. "It so happens that I have this part back at my lab, made of the correct materials with the right amount of mercury. If we're lucky, it might be compatible."

George felt hopeful once again. "When can we get it?"

"Find us some wheels, and we can go right now."

"If there's anything this junkyard has got, it's wheels," said George. "We just need to find some with an engine connected to them. C'mon, Jackbot—let's go!"

"Wait a second," Jackbot said, jumping up from his game. "What about Otto? He's going to wonder where we went."

"True," said George. "I'll leave him a note." He found a piece of paper and a pencil and quickly scribbled:

> Dear Otto,
> I'm going over to Anne's house for the afternoon—I thought I'd follow your advice and take a break from Project Mercury. I'll catch up on some schoolwork too.
> Love, George

"That should make him happy," George said, rereading the note. He turned to Cookie. "Will you deliver this to my uncle?" he asked.

Cookie looked back at Jackbot. "Perhaps we can resume our recreation at a later time?" she said.

Jackbot's eyes brightened. "Absolutely! Certainly! Most definitely!"

Cookie's eyes blinked in response. Then she took the note and glided up out of the lab.

George followed Cookie to make sure no one was around to watch them, and then led Micron, Jackbot, and the Caretaker across the yard to where Otto kept all the old smart cars that he tinkered with. The only one that still had an engine and four wheels attached was a rusty, olive-colored sedan—one of the earliest models of fully-automated cars.

"This will do splendidly," Micron said. "Let's see if we can get it started." He hopped into the driver's seat and hot-wired the ignition. Soon the engine hummed to life. "Whaddya want?" said a grouchy voice. It sounded like a disgruntled old man who'd been woken up from an afternoon nap. "Can't a car get any rest around here?"

"It's one of the old GRO-78-X Personality smart cars," Jackbot said. "They were programmed with different character traits, so you felt like the car was part of the family."

"Well, where do you want to go?" said the car peevishly. "Come on, I haven't got all day."

"The old Termite Heights bug spray factory," Micron said.

"What do you want to go there for?" said the car. "That's a bad area, you know. Nothing but thieves and vagabonds!"

"Something tells me Otto would love this car," George said.

Micron slammed the door. "Come on, everybody in!"

The Caretaker rolled up and hit the rear bumper.

"Hey! Watch the paint job, you big galoot!" said the car.

"I am too large," said the Caretaker. "Therefore, I am unable to enter the vehicle."

"You'll have to stay here then," said Micron. "Ready to go, George?"

"Hold on," said Jackbot. He tugged George's sleeve and drew him aside. "If we go without the Caretaker for protection, Micron could turn on us at any moment. Do you really think you can trust him?"

"Well . . ." George began.

"Let me answer that," Micron said from the car.

He must have ears like a bat! George thought.

"I'm about to take you to my top-secret hideout. A place that no one else—and I mean no one else—knows about. I'm trusting *you*. The least you can do is return the favor."

George looked from Micron to Jackbot and back again.

"We need that part," he pleaded to his robot friend. "It's my only hope."

Jackbot nodded. "Okay. Let's go."

"Fantastic!" Micron said, clapping his hands. George and Jackbot climbed into the back seat and closed the door. "To Termite Heights, please!" Micron said to the car.

"Whatever," the car said as it pulled out of the junk-yard. "It's your funeral."

. . .

As they drove out of town, the buildings got older and fewer until there was nothing to see but overgrown fields and dusty lots filled with tumbledown structures from long ago. Finally the car stopped in front of an enormous squat building, more dilapidated than anything else they'd seen. The few windows that weren't broken were boarded up, and paint was peeling off the walls. It had two tall brick towers, one of which had fallen in, leaving a jagged stump behind. The whole place was surrounded by a tall barbed-wire fence, but that was okay—the main gate had fallen off its hinges, so they simply drove right through.

The car came to a shuddering halt and George, Micron, and Jackbot all climbed out.

"You're welcome," said the car.

"What?" asked Micron.

"You're welcome—you know, for driving you all the way out here?"

"But . . . I didn't say thanks."

"Exactly," said the car, and switched itself off.

"They used to make bug spray here, right?" said George, as they walked to the entrance. Above the rusty steel door was a sign painted in faded red letters:

BUGS-B-GONE. Under it was a picture of a termite on its back, with *x*'s over its eyes.

"It used to be the biggest employer in town, according to my historical database," Jackbot said. "This factory was the reason it was called Termite Heights, before Droid bought up the land and built TinkerTech."

"Yes, and it was quickly abandoned," Micron said. "Making it the perfect location for my hideout. Come, let me show you!"

As they pulled the chain off the door, George thought he heard something move behind him. He spun around but saw only a bunch of scrubby-looking bushes, shivering in the breeze. The foul-smelling breeze.

"Ugh, what is that?" he asked Jackbot, pinching his nose. "It smells like rotten eggs mixed with burning rubber."

Jackbot shrugged. "I've no idea. You didn't equip me with a very well-developed olfactory system. Sadly, I am only capable of smelling French soft cheeses, old fish, and gasoline. Oh, and Otto's feet. Thanks for that."

"Oh well," said George. "It's probably nothing." They followed Micron through the door.

George expected the inside of the factory to be sleek and modern, like everything else Micron had designed —but instead, it looked exactly like the outside of the building. Shafts of light poured in through the broken windows, illuminating thick layers of dust on the floor, and cobwebs hanging from the walls. Miscellaneous robot parts lay strewn about—arms, legs, brain casings —and half-built contraptions George couldn't identify. A few old cans of bug spray were scattered around, as if Micron had never cared to clean up the place.

"Nice," said Jackbot. "Real classy."

"Come now, Jackbot," said Micron. "I bet my partner

here likes this place just fine. It's a little slice of home, isn't it, Gearing?" He gave George a chummy slap on the back. "It's strange. All that time we were working against each other—to think what we could achieve if we worked together!"

"Maybe if you hadn't been set on killing George, it would have been easier to work with him," Jackbot muttered. "Just a thought."

Micron shook his head in wonder. "A robot that can express sarcasm," he said. "I'm consistently impressed by your work with that little friend of yours, George. Of course you're right, Jackbot—I was truly rotten back then, wasn't I? But those days are behind me—and I'll prove it to you by finding the part that will help you recover your family."

While Micron was sifting through a set of metal drawers against one wall, George turned to Jackbot. "Do you have to give him such a hard time?" he asked.

"I don't like him," the robot replied, crossing his arms.

"I know, but he's helping me!"

"Is he?" said Jackbot. "Are you sure about that?"

"Got it!" Micron cried out in triumph. He walked back to George, holding a slim black device about the size of a pack of gum. "Here. It's yours." He dropped it onto George's outstretched palm.

George held the component as if it was the most precious object in the world.

"Let's go," he said to Jackbot.

"Where are we going?"

"To the lab," George said, closing his fingers around the device. "I'm getting my parents back."

The sun was low in the sky by the time
they got back to the junkyard. All the protesters were
gone. Several anti-robot signs littered the driveway.
The gate itself was locked: Otto must have gone home.
Good, George thought. *Now we won't have to worry about
sneaking around.*

"Open up, Caretaker!" George called. "We're back!"
The robot emerged from behind a shed and obediently
opened the gate with its key attachment.

Some of the robots in the yard—the few that were
still powered on—shrank back as the Caretaker led the
way to the hatch. George was shocked at their appear-
ance. These robots had been the property of Terabyte
Heights's elite—all glossy chrome, polished steel, and

flashing lights. Now they looked like they'd given up. Their metal casings were dull and tarnished, their paint was flaking, and the lights in their eyes barely flickered.

George felt guilty as he walked by them. Normally he'd never allow robots under his care to be neglected in this way. But he'd been so busy . . . *Not now,* he thought to himself. *Save your parents. Then you can save the bots!*

They reached the hatch. Micron courteously allowed George to enter first, and then he followed with Jackbot and the Caretaker.

"Have you got the device?" Micron asked.

George took it from his pocket. His heart was hammering and his mouth was dry.

"Let's hurry up and install it, then," said Micron.

George removed the old device from a tangle of wires and handed the new one to Micron. He deftly attached it, then dashed over to the central computer and entered in some commands on the display. Then he smiled and nodded. "We're ready to reboot."

George nodded back, too nervous to speak. He pulled the marble from his pocket and placed it in the hollow at the top of the central computer. The familiar low humming resumed, filling the room with noise. All of the components began beeping and flashing and clicking, and moments later, the marble glowed yellow. George reached for the activation button.

But before he could push it, a voice broke through the cacophony of sound. "I don't believe it!"

George spun around to see Anne at the bottom of the steps, staring open-mouthed at Micron, who was standing by George's side. Sparky was at her feet, a growl rumbling in his throat.

George fought off the sick feeling that was washing over him and said, "Why are you here, Anne?"

"To save you from yourself, you dimwit!" Anne shouted over the hum of the machine. "I suspected what was going on—Sparky followed you to Micron's hideout."

So that's what the awful smell was, George realized. *One of Sparky's famous farts.*

"And then I remembered the news report about the prison break—committed by a short brainy guy and a dirty little robot—and I put two and two together. You helped Micron escape and now you're working with him! How could you do it, George? After everything this lunatic has done?"

"It's not what it looks like," George said, not meeting her eyes.

"Sure it is," corrected Jackbot. "We *did* help Micron escape, and now you *are* working with him."

"Oh, all right," George said weakly. "It is what it looks like. But I had to do it—he's the only one who could repair Project Mercury. How else would I get my parents back? You'd have done the same to save your dad!"

"I'd risk *my* life to save my dad,"

Anne said. "But you are risking the lives of everyone in the whole town!"

"But there's no risk," said George. "I've been keeping an eye on him the whole time."

"Besides, I'm reformed," said Micron, smiling broadly.

"George—it's not too late. We can still call the police," said Anne.

"No!" George yelled. "I've come this far and I won't give up now!"

"Please!" Anne begged. "Listen to me!"

But George had already made up his mind. Closing his eyes, he whispered a silent prayer and pushed the button.

He kept his eyes closed, waiting for the inevitable groan of the machine as it failed at the very last minute.

He waited.

And waited.

But the noise only intensified, until the sound seemed to penetrate his entire being. He opened his eyes to see two sparkling streams of colored light exploding from the conversion pods.

"It's working!" he cried. "Anne, do you see?"

She was slowly descending the steps, and shielding her eyes from the glare.

George's limbs tingled. At any moment now he would see his parents. At any moment now, his whole life would change . . .

Then the light faded and the humming ceased, as white smoke billowed up around the chambers.

The pod doors opened with a soft hiss.

George stumbled forward. He could see the shapes

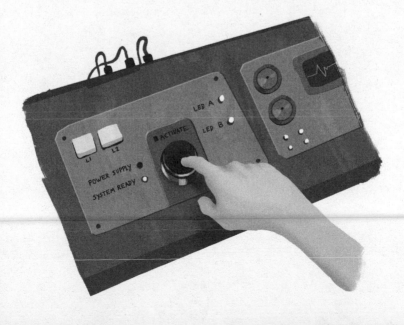

of his parents inside the chambers. "Mom?" he said. "Dad?"

"Surprise," said a voice from within the smoke. Two figures stepped out in unison.

Both of them were Charles Micron.

10

George stared, speechless with disbelief. "What—" he stammered, turning back to Micron. "What have you done?"

Micron chuckled. "*Tsk tsk.* Poor George," he said, shaking his head. "You should have listened to your friends." Anne, red-faced with rage, was glaring at Micron. Sparky was barking angrily. The robot dog went to jump at one of the clones, but Anne held him back, waiting to see what would happen next.

Micron went to stand between the two clones. They were almost exact duplicates of him, except they looked a few years younger, with no gray in their hair, and instead of the orange prison uniform Micron was still wearing, they were dressed in sharp-looking black suits.

"Gentlemen, you're looking well," said Micron.

"Hi, Chip!" said the two clones.

The original Micron smiled, showing off his perfect white teeth. "George, you seem unhappy," he said, casting a glance back at him. "Look on the bright side! It's a bad day for you, but for me—everything is coming up Micron! My plan has worked out perfectly. Surely you can feel a *little* happy for me?"

"But—how?" George said, still unable to take his eyes off the clones.

"That's what I like about you, George," Micron said. "You're always interested in the details. Well, it's very simple, you see. I was still working with your parents when they initially developed the theory of how to convert organic matter into binary data. They practiced on themselves, converting all of their genetic makeup to data and storing a copy of it on the Mercury network. At the time I thought, 'Hey, that's a pretty good idea,' and I did the same with my own data. Without telling them, of course. After all, no computer engineer works without a backup!

"Unfortunately, I never got a chance to do anything with it because they shut me out of Project Mercury after that. And then of course the machine got destroyed —until you kindly came along and rebuilt it for me." He winked. "Thanks, George, I owe you one! So once we got the whole thing going again with the component from my lab, I merely told the computer to replicate my data instead of theirs. Easy!"

While Micron was talking, George was gradually recovering from shock. He wasn't beaten yet. He still had one card to play.

"Caretaker," he said, "get Micron! Now!"

The big robot rolled forward out of the shadows and scanned the three Microns, his yellow eyes flashing with confusion. "Which one?"

"Ugh—that one!" said George, pointing to the original.

The Caretaker glided toward Micron, its steel arms outstretched.

But before the robot could reach him, Micron whipped a small black device from his pocket. He pressed a button, and a ray of white light shot out and hit the Caretaker square in the chest.

Blue ripples of electricity danced over the robot like miniature lightning bolts. The Caretaker shook violently, black smoke spilling from its head. Sparky began barking again, and Anne had to hold him back from attacking Micron. After a few seconds, the Caretaker went limp and the light faded from its eyes.

"Pretty neat, huh?" Micron said, flipping the device around his fingers. "I picked it up from my lab while we were there. One of my favorite little inventions—a handheld EMP shocker. Sleek, discreet, and powerful enough to stop a charging robot with a single zap!"

Anne finally got Sparky under control, and looked up at Micron with determination in her eyes. "You'll never get away with this!" she said.

"Dear Miss Droid, I'd love to listen to your collection of clichés someday," he said with obvious disdain. "But right now I have more important things to do. So many Microns, so little time!"

He pushed the activation button again. "No!" George

shouted, realizing what he was doing. But it was too late. The Mercury machine was humming again; the sparkling streams of light reappeared, and within seconds the conversion chambers opened up and two more Micron copies stepped out.

Then two more.

And two more after that.

Soon, the lab was crowded with Micron clones, at least thirty. They all greeted each other and shook hands. "Hey, Chip!"

"Chip! How's it going?"

"Looking good, Chip!"

"You too, Chip!"

"We need to get out of here," Jackbot whispered into George's ear. "*Now.*"

George nodded. He began sidling toward the exit, pulling Anne along with him.

The original Micron looked away from the clones and spotted them inching toward the steps. "Stop them, Chips!" he shouted.

George ducked under the arm of one Micron and dodged around another. His feet hit the metal steps, and he was halfway up before more Microns grabbed him by the shoulders and dragged him back into the lab. They turned him around, and George's heart fell as he saw that Anne hadn't gotten very far either. Two more Microns were holding her by both arms.

"Unhand them, villains!" Jackbot shouted, and launched a flying drop kick at one of the three Microns who were holding George. His flat metal feet connected with the clone's square jaw, and they both crashed to the floor.

But just as Jackbot was getting up, a ray of light connected with his chest and tossed the little robot back to the ground like a rag doll. "Mi-cronnnnnnnnnn!"

Jackbot cried, as fingers of blue lightning rippled over his body. And then he was still.

"Bull's eye!" Dr. Micron said, putting the EMP shocker back in his pocket.

"Jackbot!" George said. "Are you all right?" He struggled to break free and run to his friend, but two of the clones still held him fast.

"It's so touching, the way you care about that heap of scrap metal," Micron said. "Don't worry—I only gave him a short blast. He'll live to annoy another day. Anyway, I want that smart-aleck robot to see the next phase of my master plan!" He opened up the main panel of the central computer, disconnected the CPU, and handed it to one of the clones for safekeeping.

"What are you doing with that?" George demanded.

"You'll see," Micron said with a grin. "All right, boys," he called out to the gang of clones. "Pack it up and hit the road! And let's keep a low profile, shall we? The Terabyte Heights police force is undoubtedly looking for me—and I'd rather they didn't find that I've multiplied since my escape from prison. Don't want to spoil the surprise, do we?"

"Sure thing, Chip!"

"Happy to oblige, Chip!"

"We're on it, Chip!"

They dragged George and Anne out of the laboratory and up the steps through the hatch. Behind them, one of the Microns carried Jackbot.

The abandoned robots roused themselves from their stupor to check out what was going on. A dozen of them approached when they saw Jackbot.

"What happened to him?" a butler-bot asked.

"Okay he is?" HP said.

"He's been zapped," Dr. Micron snapped, "and if you buckets of bolts don't back off, you'll get the same!" He brandished the EMP weapon and the robots retreated.

One of the clones had commandeered Otto's truck, and the other Microns were climbing into it. "Throw these two kids in the back," said Dr. Micron. "And the little robot too."

As the clone that carried Jackbot moved toward the

truck, Cookie suddenly broke from the ranks of the yard robots and flew toward him.

"But you can't take him!" she exclaimed. "We never finished our chess game . . ."

"I said, back off!" Dr. Micron snarled, and zapped Cookie with a short blast from the shocker. She fell to the ground, raising a small cloud of dust. George thought she had been shut down, but in a last effort, Cookie extended a slender silver arm to try to grasp onto the clone's pant leg. But he kicked her arm away, sending the little robot spinning into the corner of the junkyard. This time, she didn't move.

George stared at her in wonder. Had she actually developed *feelings* for Jackbot? That was impossible. Only Jackbot had programming that advanced — unless, somehow, Cookie had *learned* to feel?

But before George could finish thinking about this, the clones swung him into the truck. He landed on the hard metal floor with a thump. A moment later Anne was thrown in too, along with the limp form of Jackbot who clattered down beside them. Once the Microns had chained their ankles to metal posts on the floor of the truck, the clones tossed the tarp over the three, covering them in darkness.

After a lot of banging and grumbling from the clones all trying to fit up front, some of them decided they had to ride in the frumpy old smart car instead. The sedan was less than thrilled—George could hear it grumbling. A few minutes later, the engine roared to life and the truck began to move.

As it picked up speed, George thought he heard a dog barking.

"That's Sparky!" said Anne. "He must be following us!"

But a few seconds later, the barking died away.

"I guess he couldn't keep up," Anne said, her voice somber.

"It's going to be okay," George said into the gloom. "Just like you said. Right, Anne?"

But Anne didn't reply.

If George had thought he felt lonely before, it was

nothing compared to this moment. And the situation was entirely his fault.

Many minutes later, the truck came to a stop. The tarp that covered them was thrown back, revealing the night sky, twinkling with stars. One of the Micron clones loomed over them.

"Nap's over," it said.

George climbed stiffly down, then held out his hand to help Anne from the truck. She ignored him and got out by herself.

They were standing in front of the BUGS-B-GONE building.

"Welcome back to my top-secret hideout!" Dr. Micron said. He glanced over at one of the clones with a smirk. "I love saying that."

"It's not a secret now that we know about it," Anne pointed out.

"Ugh," Micron groaned, rolling his eyes. "You Droids are all alike—no fun at all! Anyway, neither of you will be in the business of telling secrets for long. Now, enough small talk. Pick up that robot and follow me!"

One of the clones gathered Jackbot in his arms and pulled him down from the truck. A platoon of Microns surrounded George and Anne and marched them into the building.

Inside, everything looked as drab and dusty as before. The clone dropped Jackbot at George's feet with a clatter.

"Hey!" George protested. "Be careful!"

Jackbot sat up and rubbed his head. "Way to kick a robot when he's down," he muttered. His eyes flickered, and took in his surroundings. "Oh, no. This dump again?"

"Dump?" Micron said. "Well, that's only because you didn't see the place at its best. Behold!" He opened a metal panel in the wall to reveal a small console, lined with buttons and flashing lights. His fingers danced over the controls, and then—everything changed.

The walls squealed on invisible hinges and opened up to reveal vistas of computer banks, monitors, and other devices—a gleaming landscape of high-tech equipment.

A section of the dust-covered floor rolled back and hydraulic platforms rose up, carrying even more shining machines. Within moments, the whole space was transformed into a state-of-the-art laboratory, a far cry from the grubby, half-empty area Micron had shown them before.

Just like his office at TinkerTech, George thought. *Everything that matters is kept secret and out of sight.*

In fact, it was all a bit like Micron himself: flashy and arrogant.

Sleek LCD displays descended from the ceiling. Some showed aerial views of Terabyte Heights; others featured diagrams and blueprints of robots and other inventions not even George could identify.

"Pretty neat, huh?" Micron said. "The word 'genius' is overused, of course, but I feel in my case—"

"Why are you doing all this?" George blurted out. "I don't get it. You had one of the best jobs in the world at TinkerTech. You could have developed all of these inventions there! Why do it all in secret? Why become a criminal?"

The smug grin fell from Micron's face, and he turned to George. "You want to know why, George Gearing? Fine. I'll tell you. All my working life I've been plagued by people who thought they were smarter than me. First, it was that bumbling idiot Droid—"

"Hey!" shouted Anne.

"Pardon me," Micron said. "I should have said, that bumbling idiot *Professor* Droid. From the day I started

working at TinkerTech, the man did everything he could to shut down my most revolutionary ideas in the name of 'humanity' and 'morality.' All that time—wasted! Then the Gearings came along—two young people with big ideas—and I thought I could mold them to my own image. But no! They betrayed me as well—shut me out because they couldn't see the big picture. And now *you*, Gearing—a punk kid and his nosy friend and that pile of recycled processors you call a robot—showing up again and again to ruin my plans! I'm tired of playing second fiddle to people who wouldn't know what to do with real *power* if you handed it to them on a silver platter. Some of us are natural rulers, George. And make no mistake: I intend to rule!"

Micron turned to a screen that displayed a blueprint of a complicated-looking robot. He touched the screen, then swiped his arm up into the air with a flourish. The image leaped right off the display. It grew into a massive 3D hologram, projected into the center of the room. As it slowly rotated, both George and Anne gasped.

It looked like a giant metal spider. It had eight jointed legs, a bulbous body with a control center at the top, and a small round head with pincer-like jaws. The control platform was equipped with a dozen steel tubes that stuck out like gun barrels.

"Quite a piece of work, isn't it?" said Micron, gazing at it with pride. "I call it the Spider—in honor of this insect-spray factory where it was designed."

"Technically, spiders aren't insects," Jackbot piped up. "They have eight legs, not six. Therefore they belong to the order Arachnidae—"

"And technically I could have my replicated friends here take you apart and rebuild you as a toaster," Micron interrupted. "But I won't do that just yet, unless you keep running your metal mouth! Now, where was I? Oh, yes. I designed the Spider some time ago—and if my original plan had worked out, the good people of Terabyte Heights would have built it for me when they were under the influence of my MOD devices. Well, you ruined that one for me, George. But that's okay, because now I have a better plan. First, I used the machine you so kindly rebuilt to make all of these copies of wonderful me!"

The Micron clones all congratulated themselves and straightened their ties.

"These fine fellows will build the Spider in no time. But listen, it gets better! When I first designed the Spider, it was simply going to be a giant scary robot that fired lasers at people. Not bad, but a little crude. Now I have a better idea. I'm going to fit the CPU from

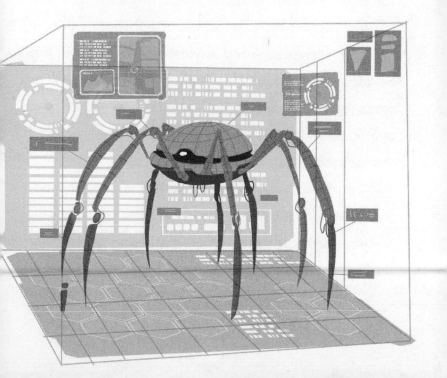

Project Mercury into the Spider! Instead of firing regular old lasers, its beam will turn people into pure data! Just like that! I'll start by digitizing everyone in Terabyte Heights. Imagine—all those thousands of people contained in tiny little chips you can hold in the palm of your hand! What a demonstration of power! After that, when I pick up the phone and call the president of the United States, he'll do whatever I want or I'll digitize him too. Better yet, maybe he'll do whatever I want, and I'll digitize him anyway! I can rule the whole world! Emperor of Earth! That has a nice ring to it, no?" He laughed maniacally. "The whole of humanity will bow before my greatness—and anyone who doesn't will just be zapped into binary oblivion! Who needs prisons when you've got hard drives? You don't have to feed ones and zeros, and there's no way to escape!"

"He's totally insane," Anne muttered.

"A nutjob," Jackbot agreed. "A fruit loop. One sandwich short of a picnic."

"I am perfectly sane!" Micron said angrily. His face flushed a dull red. "You won't be laughing when I've digitized you! But I'll leave you for last. I want you to watch me digitize the whole town first. Chips?"

"Yes, Chip?"

"Here, Chip."

"What can we do for you, Chip?"

"Put these two insolent kids and this rude robot in the cage, would you?"

"Right away, Chip!"

"No problem, Chip!"

"Consider it done, Chip!"

Several of the clones grabbed George, Anne, and Jackbot by the arms and tossed them into a steel enclosure in the corner of the room.

The lock clicked shut.

11

Throughout the night, the lab was busier than a beehive. The Microns swarmed around the room, working nonstop to construct the enormous Spider-bot. The hologram had been deactivated, but was rapidly being replaced by the real thing. George watched with a dull ache in his stomach as the clones ran to and fro, shouting instructions and assembling metal pieces and drilling and hammering and generally making a mighty ruckus. The body was already in place and now the huge, jointed legs were being attached by clones wielding blowtorches. For the most part they worked in perfect harmony, as if they were multiple extensions of the villain's consciousness.

Only occasionally did they demonstrate signs of

independent thought, most often when there was a question of who was actually in charge. They seemed to be having some difficulty agreeing on the chain of command, and kept bickering among themselves.

"Bring me that adjustable wrench, Chip!"

"Can't you see I'm busy? Get it yourself!"

"If we weren't so handsome, I'd smack you right in that gorgeous face of yours!"

"Well! *Some*one got up on the wrong side of the conversion chamber, didn't he?"

"*Will you please stop squabbling!*" Dr. Micron sputtered. "You, over there—*no, the other one!* Give him the wrench!"

And so the work continued. Soon the Spider-bot would be complete. Micron's master plan was in motion.

And from behind the reinforced bars of the cage, George couldn't think of a single way to stop him.

If Micron takes over the world, it will be because of me, he thought.

"Anne," George said suddenly. "I want you to know that I'm really, really sorry. I should have listened to you. I should have told you what I was planning with Micron—"

Anne looked up from where she was slumped in the corner of the cage, her face set in an angry glare. "Then why didn't you?"

"I thought—I thought you'd say I was being crazy. That you'd try to stop me—"

"You *were* being crazy, and I *would* have stopped you!" said Anne. "That's the point, Robot Boy. That's what friends are for! To stop you from doing stupid things like breaking criminal masterminds out of high-security prisons and working with them to create weapons of mass destruction!"

"When you put it that way, it does sound bad," George said miserably.

Anne's eyes softened and she sighed. "Oh, wipe that hangdog look off your face. It's impossible to stay mad at you. With your messy hair and your rumpled clothes—"

"If only Cookie were here, she'd fix him right up,"

Jackbot moaned. "Where's a beautiful grooming-bot when you need one?"

Anne laughed for the first time in hours. "Look, what's done is done. I accept your apology, and your offer to do my homework for the rest of the school year."

"But, I didn't—" George stuttered.

"I'm ready to move past this. And there's no time to waste—we've got a town to save!" She held out her hand to George and he grasped it. "Friends?" she asked.

George grinned. "Always," he replied.

"This is just *so* touching," Jackbot said, flapping at his eyes with his claw. "Okay, Jackbot, hold it together, hold it together!"

"Yes, please," George added, "I need you focused."

"So!" Anne said, getting to her feet. "How do we get out of here? Can you bend those bars, Jackbot?"

Jackbot scanned the bars and shook his head. "Nope, that's solid titanium. We'd need some serious plastic explosives to blast through those. And given our proximity, plastic explosives would blast us as well."

"There's a lock on the outside," Anne said, snaking her arm between the bars. She gave up after a few tries. "Darn! I can't reach it."

"What are you three whispering about?" said Micron, strolling over toward them. "Plotting your daring escape? It's no use. I've won. The Spider's complete and we're about to take it for a test drive. You don't want to miss this!"

George peered through the cage bars and saw the hulking shape of the Spider looming above them—thirty feet tall and bristling with legs the size of tree trunks.

"If only we had a really, really big boot," Jackbot muttered. *"Splat!"*

"Sorry, we're fresh out of planet-size boots," Anne replied. "We'll have to think of another way to stop it."

"Picky, picky."

The Micron clones were practically dancing with excitement as they prepared for the test. One of them placed a small wire cage with a rat inside in front of the Spider.

"Okay," Dr. Micron said. "Activate!"

"I'll do it!" said a clone that was standing on the Spider's back.

"Hey! You said if I let you attach the last leg, *I* could shoot the rodent!" said another clone.

They're all crazed with power like the original, George thought. *Every one of them wants to be the boss!*

"Enough!" Micron shouted. "If you keep it up, when this is over I'm deactivating all of you; I don't care *how* handsome you are."

The clones quieted, grumbling unhappily.

"That's better. Now, you up there on the platform —activate!"

The clone pushed a lever, and a moment later the Spider's massive head turned, zeroing in with its eight blood-red eyes on the caged rat. As if sensing something bad was about to happen, the rat started scampering frantically around the cage.

A halo of white light shone from the barrel of one of the Spider's laser guns an instant before a beam shot across the room—striking the cage. George watched in horror as the tail of the rat disassembled into thousands of motes of light, then its body, and finally its head. The last George saw of the rat was its bulging pink eyes —looking utterly confused. And then it was gone.

The clones cheered.

"Nice work, lads!" said Dr. Micron. He whipped out a small pad of paper from his pocket with the words "To Do" printed on the top and studied it. "Okay, build and test terrifying war machine—check. So, the next thing is to digitize the entire population of Terabyte Heights . . ." He picked up a pencil from a nearby table and chewed on the end of it thoughtfully. "And then world domination after lunch. Fantastic!" Micron looked down at his orange jumpsuit in distaste. "Hmm. I think I'd better change first, don't you? It simply wouldn't do for an evil genius to conquer the world in prison clothes. Ah! I have just the thing in my closet downstairs. Talk amongst yourselves while I'm gone!" He dashed from the lab with a spring in his step.

George turned back to his friends. "We don't have

much time—we've got to get out of here and warn everyone in town!"

"But how?" Jackbot asked. "I have been running the numbers, and we have an infinitesimally small chance of escaping this cage. Unless we had a can of hair spray, some fake vomit, and a roll of salami."

George and Anne stared at Jackbot for a long time.

"I don't even want to know," George finally said.

"Listen!" said Anne suddenly. "Hear that?"

George listened hard, and heard the distant sound of a dog barking.

"It's Sparky!" said Anne. "He must have found us after all!"

"If he can get into the factory, he can open the cage from the outside!" said George.

"Yeah, but do you think the Microns will stand by and let that happen?" Jackbot asked.

"They might," said Anne. A sly grin spread across her face. "We just need a little diversion. Follow my lead." She walked to the front of the cage and rattled the bars.

"Hey, Microns! Your Spider machine—how do you know if it even works on humans?"

The clones all turned to look at Anne.

"It worked on the rat," said one.

"Well, sure—but a human is light years more complicated than a rat!" Anne scoffed. "Much more data to store!"

"The Spider works on *any* biological matter," said another clone, crossing his arms. "Rat, human, elephant—it doesn't matter."

"Uh-huh. Big words for a bunch of second-rate copies of a second-rate robotics engineer. I'll believe that when I see it!"

The Microns muttered angrily in response, and George could see they were getting more agitated by the minute.

But Anne persisted. "Admit it!" she said. "You're afraid it won't work! That all of this will be for nothing, and that by the end of the day you'll be turned back into a bunch of ones and zeros!" She shook her head in disgust. "A big machine like this and no human trials.

154

Good luck with that, guys!" One of the clones nudged another one, saying, "Why don't we try it out on her? That'll shut her up!"

"Hah!" said Anne. "You don't have the guts."

George shot her a startled look. *What's she planning?* he wondered anxiously.

"Anyway," Anne continued, "you can't make decisions for yourselves without the real Dr. Micron."

"We're as real as he is!" said a different clone. "Every one of us!"

"Which one's in charge, then?" George demanded. He began to see where Anne was going with this.

"Me, of course," said one of them. "I was the first out of the machine, so I'm closest to the original."

"Hardly!" said another. "I was the last one out of the machine, so I'm obviously the most up-to-date model!"

"But my jawline is clearly more chiseled than yours!" said another.

"I'm in charge!"

"No, me!"

George didn't know which clone threw the first

punch, but within seconds the scene had deteriorated into an all-out brawl. Dozens of Microns were pummeling one another and shouting at the tops of their lungs that they, and none of the others, were the best Micron of all.

"Look!" George said, and pointed to a broken window nearby. Sparky's little metal head was peeking through, searching the room for his beloved owner.

"Sparky!" Anne called out. "Here, boy!" She tapped the bars of the cage, and Sparky hopped through the window and ran to her, tail wagging. "Now open that door!"

The robot-dog gripped the lock in his iron jaws and crunched down. A moment later, Sparky dropped the lock's mangled remains on the ground and the cage door swung open.

"Good boy!" said Anne. She ran from the cage and patted the dog. "When we get home, you can chew up *all* of Daddy's shoes!"

George peered out at the clones. They hadn't yet

noticed. "So far, so good," he said. "But we still need a way to get back to Terabyte Heights! We're at least ten miles from town."

"We'll figure it out later," Anne said. "For now, let's get out of here!" She turned and followed Sparky back to the window. Sparky hopped outside, his spring-loaded legs making the jump in one effortless leap.

"You next, Jackbot," George said. "You're the small-est, so we'll give you a leg up." George heaved the little robot up. Jackbot sailed through the window, and a moment later George heard a crash from outside.

"I'm okay!" Jackbot called out. "Just a dent or two! Or . . . seven!"

Anne winced. "Do you think he's all right?"

George grinned. "Believe me, he's had worse."

He was about to give Anne a leg up as well when they suddenly realized the room was a lot quieter than before. Swallowing hard, George and Anne turned around and saw the eyes of every Micron clone trained on them.

"Uh-oh," Anne said.

"Get them!" one of the clones shouted. He had a black eye and his suit jacket was torn.

The entire army of clones began advancing on them.

"There's nowhere to run!" George cried, looking desperately for an escape route. But they were surrounded.

"Do you think Micron Number One will mind if we maim them just a little?" one of the clones asked.

"I wouldn't, if I were him," said another. "Oh wait, I am!"

Anne glanced over at George. "Well, Robot Boy, it's been nice knowing you . . ."

George nodded, retreating until his back was against the wall.

An instant later, the world exploded. George and Anne dived aside as Otto's truck came barreling through the wall next to them, scattering Microns like bowling pins. Through the cloud of billowing brick dust, George saw the small square face of Jackbot peering over the dashboard from the driver's seat.

"How about that for a grand entrance?" shouted Jackbot.

George leaped to his feet and sprinted to the truck, with Anne by his side holding Sparky. They threw themselves into the cabin and Jackbot lurched the truck into reverse. George saw that Jackbot had strapped two cans of bug spray to his feet so he could reach the pedals.

Amid the swirling dust inside the factory, the original Micron appeared, now wearing a white tuxedo and a bow tie, with a red carnation in his lapel. "What the—?" he exclaimed, surveying the damage. Then he spied the truck. "You stupid fools!" he shouted at the clones. "They're getting away! Stop them at once!"

The army of Microns ran toward the truck. Jackbot backed out of the crumpled wall at top speed, yanked up the hand brake, and spun the truck around. George's back slammed against the seat as Jackbot hit the gas, and the clones disappeared behind them as the truck sped away.

SMASH!

The truck broke through the front gate like it was made of matchsticks. And then the escaped prisoners were roaring down the road toward Terabyte Heights.

"Jackbot, that was amazing!" George exclaimed. He had never felt more proud of his friend. "I didn't know you could drive!"

"Neither did I!" Jackbot replied. He hit a mailbox by the side of the road and sent it flying, then managed to wrestle the truck back onto the pavement. "My bad!" he shouted out the window.

"So now we get back to town, tell the cops about Micron's latest plot, and put him back where he belongs —in prison!" said Anne. "We won!"

"Yeah!" said George. *And when I get back to the lab,* he thought, *I can use the machine to finally get my parents back!* But no sooner had that thought crossed his mind that he became aware of a strange noise. It sounded far away but was getting louder quickly. "Can you guys hear a sort of—clomping sound?"

"What, like—a horse?" said Anne.

"Bigger than that," George said. "Sort of like an

elephant, only with more legs . . ." George's voice trailed off as the reality dawned on him. Glancing up at the rear-view mirror, he saw that what he'd feared was true.

There, not too far behind them, the giant silver Spider was stamping down the center of the road. Each step shook the ground beneath its feet.

George felt the blood drain from his face. "Maybe we were a little premature on that whole winning thing."

12

"Step on it!" George shouted.

"I *am* stepping on it!" Jackbot shouted back.

"JUST GO FASTER!"

"It's gaining on us!" Anne yelled, craning her neck.

Sparky had his head stuck out the passenger side window, his tongue lolling in the wind. Jackbot glanced over at him. "Well, at least *someone* is enjoying himself."

Moments later they hit the edge of town, shops and houses beginning to line the road. Half a dozen cars were stopped at a traffic light, and Jackbot slammed on the brakes, screeching to a sudden halt right behind them in a cloud of exhaust.

Through the back window, George saw the Spider stomping steadily toward them. Dozens of black-suited

Microns stood on its back on the control platform, the wind blowing through their hair, and the remaining clones were stationed one to each of the Spider's eight huge legs, riding along near the ground. At the front of the platform stood Dr. Micron in his pristine white tuxedo, his head proudly raised and his arms folded across his chest.

George hit the horn, but the traffic didn't budge.

"Everyone out of the truck!" George said. "We have to get into town and warn people before it's too late!"

Jackbot switched off the engine and they all jumped down onto the sidewalk and dashed toward the center of town, where people were peacefully going about their business.

"Everybody run!" George shouted at the people on the streets, shattering the tranquil scene. "A huge Spider is coming and the whole town is in imminent danger!"

Everyone stopped in their tracks and stared.

"A huge spider, eh?" a construction worker said, chuckling. He pulled a newspaper off a stack on the street corner and rolled it up. "Don't worry, kid. I can take care of it for you."

A moment later the Spider came into view, its enormous, glittering bulk casting a long shadow across the street and the pedestrians. One of its legs came down on Otto's truck with an earsplitting crunch, sending shattered glass and twisted metal flying through the air.

Glancing at the construction worker, whose jaw was hanging open, George leaned over and said, "I think you're going to need a bigger newspaper."

And that's when everyone started screaming.

People dropped what they were carrying and fled, scattering in all directions. But among the screams George heard a very strange sound: laughter. Looking up, he saw that it was Micron himself, grinning from ear to ear as he looked down upon the town below. He must have been wearing a microphone, because the sound was distorted and amplified. "You can run, friends!" he shouted. "But you cannot hide!"

A ray of blinding white light shot from one of the Spider's laser cannons and struck a man in a three-piece suit, who had been so engrossed in a phone call that he didn't notice the chaos all around him. His feet dissolved first, then his legs and his torso, until all that was left was the hand holding the phone and his puzzled face, saying, "Marsha? Marsha? Let me call you back—" And then he was gone.

Within seconds, a dozen more had been digitized, and the air was alive with flashes of light and cries of fear, rays hitting people in their backs as they ran.

"We've got to hide!" George shouted above the din.

"Quick! Over here in the alley!" He motioned for Anne and Jackbot to follow him into the narrow space between the grocery store and the bank. But Sparky wasn't with them. The robot dog had run out into the middle of the street and was barking furiously at the Spider. The monster's multiple eyes zeroed in on the little dog.

"Sparky, no!" Anne cried.

ZAP!

For a second, Sparky was engulfed in an explosion of light. But when the light faded, George saw that Sparky was left standing in the exact same spot—barking as if nothing at all had happened.

"Oh, thank goodness," Anne sighed. "Come, Sparky! Here, boy!" The robot dog padded into the alley and licked Anne's face.

"Look at him," George exclaimed in wonder. "He's perfectly fine!"

Jackbot looked thoughtful. "Project Mercury," he mused. "It only works on organic matter, right? So it has no effect on robots!"

"You're right!" George said.

Suddenly a voice boomed down from above. George looked up to see Dr. Micron peering down on them from his perch atop the Spider's back. He smiled.

"So glad I caught up with you, George," Micron said. "I hope you've enjoyed seeing the fruits of your labor. Now—prepare for oblivion!"

One of the Spider's laser cannons swiveled and fixed on him.

George dived to one side as the digitizing ray shot out, striking the ground where he'd been standing. "Go! Go! Go!" he shouted, and they all sprinted through the alley and onto the street behind it.

"Now what?" Anne asked, panting.

George looked up the street. "The middle school isn't far from here!" he said. "We can warn the others and hide in the building!"

"Ugh," Anne grumbled. "On top of everything else that's happened today, we have to go to *school?*"

George shrugged. "It's that or oblivion."

Anne screwed up her face in thought. "It's a tough call," she said. "But okay. Let's go to school."

Jackbot led the way through a maze of back streets and alleys, trying to avoid being spotted by Micron and his clones. After a few narrow escapes, they finally saw the gate to the school straight ahead. They burst in through the double doors, startling Mr. Cog, who was mopping the linoleum like it was just another day.

"George!" Mr. Cog exclaimed, hand pressed to his chest. "You scared me half to death! What are you doing here? I thought you had some sort of unpleasant rash on your rear and had to stay home."

George stared at him. "A rash on my *what?*"

"Your posterior. Your tail end. You know. At least that's what the secretary told me your uncle said."

George closed his eyes. "If we survive this," he said to Anne, "remind me to kill Otto."

Mr. Cog's eyebrows furrowed. "Survive *what?*"

"Dr. Micron's back!" Anne replied. "He's made a bunch of copies of himself, and now he and his army of clones are riding a giant spider through town and zapping everyone with digitizing laser guns!"

Mr. Cog nodded calmly, looking for all the world

as if she'd told him there was a mess in the cafeteria. "Well," he said, hitching up his pants, "I knew this day would come." Mop in hand, he spun it around and yanked the dripping head from the end of it, dropping it to the ground with a splat. He then whirled the mop stick through the air like a ninja, and struck the glass-protected fire alarm on the wall behind him. At once, alarms began to blare throughout the school.

"What—how did you—" George stammered.

Mr. Cog straightened up and gave a stiff bow. "Black belt in karate and aikido," he said with a wink. "That Caretaker fellow has nothing on me."

The door of Principal Qwerty's office burst open and she marched out, tight-lipped and frowning. "What in the world is going on here?"

"The town is under attack!" George said. "Is there some kind of bomb shelter in the basement? Do you have a direct line to the military?"

"Slow down, Gearing!" said the principal, struggling to be heard over the alarm. "You are supposed to be at home in bed, mister! Furthermore, why have you brought these robots to school?"

George hesitated. He hardly knew where to begin.

"Explain yourself, young man!"

"Listen, lady," Anne broke in. "That thing is headed right this way. Do what he says!"

"I will not be spoken to in that way!" the principal railed. "I . . . what's that noise?"

Everyone got quiet.

Boom. Boom. Boom. The water in Mr. Cog's mopping pail trembled.

"I'm going to get to the bottom of this," Principal

Qwerty grumbled, and pushed through the doors to go outside. About five seconds later, she came back through the doors like a flash, and slammed them behind her. "The town is under attack!" she screeched.

"That's what he's been trying to tell you!" said Anne.

"Evacuate!" the principal screamed. "Evacuate!" She ran down the corridor banging on classroom doors. "Everyone out! Leave through the back entrance!"

"No, no, no!" George shouted. "If you go out there, you'll be zapped! You've got to stay inside the building!" But George's pleas went unheard. Soon the corridors and hallways were filled with panicked students and teachers, all of them streaming toward the rear of the school.

"What do we do now?" Jackbot asked.

"I don't know," George said, watching hopelessly. "I thought we could warn everyone, but all we did was make things worse!"

"Come on!" Anne said. "Maybe it's not too late to stop them!" She ran out after the crowd, and George, Jackbot, and Sparky took off after her. Outside, the

students were huddled in groups with their teachers next to the building. Principal Qwerty was yelling into her phone. "Yes!" she shouted. "The fire department! The police! We need them here right now! What? What do you mean they've all been zapped?"

Then George saw the Spider. It was stalking around the side of the school, looking over the trees that lined the baseball field, searching. Everyone went deathly still.

"What is that thing?" Patricia Volt whispered, having arrived at George's side. "This is your fault, isn't it?"

George swallowed hard. "It's Dr. Micron's latest invention! It converts everyone into data—and yeah . . . this time, it *is* my fault."

"Converting everyone into data?" said Patricia. "What are you talking about, Gearing?"

The Spider turned its head toward them. White light shot from its laser and struck Principal Qwerty. Everyone watched, horrified, as she disappeared into a million points of light.

"That's what I'm talking about!" George shouted to Patricia.

Patricia's face went white. "Is she . . . dead?"

"No, just downloaded onto Micron's massive hard drive!" George said. "In theory, she could be brought back, but—"

Then—pandemonium. Kids and teachers began running in all directions, hotly pursued by the giant metal robot. Lasers shot from its head, digitizing them as they fled.

"George Gearing!" Dr. Micron boomed. "Peek-a-boo! Prepare to go digital!"

One of the Spider's laser cannons was aimed at George's chest.

George stared up at the ray, frozen to the spot. He knew he should dive for cover, but he was tired of running, so tired. And the situation was hopeless. How could one person stop such a powerful machine? The whole town was going to become a series of ones and zeros, and it was all because of him. He felt like the biggest zero of all. Giving up would be a relief.

At the last second, something slammed into his side, shoving him to the ground. Dazed, he saw Patricia as the ray hit her instead of George. He gasped as her brand-new high-tops vanished into particles, then her designer jeans, as the wave of digitization moved swiftly up her torso.

"I—I don't understand," George stammered. "You hate my guts!"

"You may be a loser," Patricia said, her eyes wide with fear. "But you're the only loser smart enough to save Terabyte Heights." Her face began to dissolve.

"I don't know how!" George protested.

But she was gone.

George stared at the place where Patricia had just been, his mind blank. Anne pulled at his sleeve. "George! George, we have to get out of here — or Patricia will have sacrificed herself for nothing!"

Bending low, George followed Anne, Jackbot, and Sparky across the field, dodging Micron's attack. The Spider was glowing with laser beams, and students and teachers were vanishing all around them. Somehow the four friends made it to the gate, with the Spider bearing down on them.

George sighed with relief as he saw the school bus, driven by Mr. Cog, screech to a halt on the road outside. "Jump in!" the janitor shouted. They scrambled aboard and Mr. Cog drove off at top speed before he'd even closed the door.

As the bus roared through the nearly empty streets of Terabyte Heights, Mr. Cog swung left and right whenever he could, trying to keep out of the Spider's direct line of sight. The last of the citizens fleeing on foot disappeared one by one into Micron's massive hard drive.

"Where to now?" Mr. Cog asked.

George scoured his mind for an answer. *Patricia saved me so I could stop Micron — but how?* Sparky jumped up on the seat beside him and licked George's face with his rubbery silicon tongue. "Thanks, Sparky," George said, rubbing him behind the ears. "At least you survived the digitizing ray." And as soon as the words left his mouth, a plan began to take shape in George's mind.

He'd need an army to bring down the Spider, and humans were defenseless in the face of Micron's creation.

But Sparky had survived the ray because he was robotic.

And George knew exactly where to find an army of robots.

"We have to get to my uncle's junkyard!" he told Mr. Cog. "Step on it!"

Otto dashed out of his office the moment the bus careened through the junkyard gate. "George!" Otto exclaimed, spotting his face through the window. "I've been worried sick! Terabyte Heights is under siege and you're off gallivanting around town in a school bus. You weren't even supposed to *be* at school today!"

"I'm sorry, Otto," George said as he and his friends jumped off the bus. "But can you punish me later? Right now we've got to stop Micron!"

"Micron?" Otto spluttered. "I might have known that worm was behind all this! How did he get out of prison, anyhow?"

George groaned. "I'll explain later."

"I'm heading back into town!" Mr. Cog said, standing in the door of the bus. "I'll see if I can rescue anyone else before it's too late!"

"It's too dangerous!" Anne said.

Mr. Cog picked up his mop stick from the floor and gripped it. "Well, if I go down, I'm going to take a few of them with me!"

George nodded at the janitor with respect. "Good luck out there, Mr. Cog," he said.

The janitor gave another stiff bow, jumped into the

driver's seat, and backed the bus out of the junkyard. Then he careened off in a cloud of dust.

"Let's get into Otto's office," George said. "We don't want to be out in the open if the Spider comes this way." Inside, a battered old television was broadcasting the local news at high volume. Onscreen, a grave-looking news anchor with long black hair was narrating live footage from the streets of Terabyte Heights.

"Hundreds of people have already been struck down by Dr. Micron's latest weapon," she announced. "It has been terrorizing the town for the past hour." The scene cut to a group of soldiers firing at the Spider. George recognized Sergeant Surge among them, the man who had stopped them near the TinkerTech HQ. Surge was shouting at his men to keep firing, but the bullets bounced harmlessly off the giant robot's metal armor. White light illuminated the TV frame, and when the light faded, all the soldiers had vanished. Then the camera clattered to the ground.

The news anchor scrambled to grab the camera and

point it toward herself. She touched a finger to her ear. George saw that her hand was shaking. "Authorities advise everyone to stay where they are, and under no circumstances to attempt to confront the attackers. Mayor Buffer has declared a state of emergency—" She stopped mid-sentence, staring in shock at something off camera. George heard muffled thuds and screams.

Seconds later a white ray of light hit the news anchor in the chest. "This is Amy Broadband for Terabyte News!" she exclaimed, as the camera hit the ground and she disappeared.

The screen went black.

Otto turned to George and Anne. "That's it, kids; you're going down to the lab, where you'll be safe." He snatched up a sledgehammer attachment from the desk and secured it to his robotic arm. "I'm not letting some big bug stomp all over *my* property!"

"Otto, wait!" George said, grabbing his uncle's arm. "Look, I'm the one who got us into this mess, and there's no way I'm going to hide underground while everyone else tries to stop Micron. I'm going back out there."

Otto grunted. "All right, kid," he sighed. "I was never able to stop you from pulling one of your crazy stunts, was I?"

"But, George," Anne said. "How are we going to fight that thing?"

George looked at Jackbot and smiled. "As it turns out, I have a plan after all."

13

Checking first to make sure they'd be okay outside, George led everyone back out into the junkyard. "I want you to rouse every single robot here," he said. "They've been in sleep mode for days, so I'm sure they'll be rested and ready the second you give them a new job to do."

"What do you need all those house-bots for?" Otto asked. "You want them to plant a garden for you or something? Vacuum a rug?"

But Anne was smiling. "I think I see what you're getting at, Robot Boy," she said. "That digitizing ray didn't work on Sparky, so you're thinking it won't work on these robots either!"

"He's correct!" Jackbot said. "It only works on organic matter—the other robots and I are immune to it!"

"Exactly," George said, nodding. "And we've got a whole army of them! C'mon, we don't have much time."

Within minutes, George and his friends had assembled all of the various robots in the center of the junkyard. "Hmm," Anne said. "They do look a bit worse for wear, don't they?"

She was right. The robots were even shabbier than before; their limbs and wheels were squeaky with neglect, and many of them were already covered with a thin layer of rust.

"Hello, robots!" George said, trying to sound cheerful. "I know you haven't had much to do for a while, but a giant robot is terrorizing the city, and we need your help to stop it!"

The robots stared miserably at George, silent. A butler-bot finally spoke up and said, "Most of us are only house-bots, George Gearing. We have no programming for combat. We are useless to you, as we were to our humans who abandoned us here."

George tried to argue with them, but it was no use. The robots began retreating back into the shadows of the junkyard.

"I don't get it," Anne said. "I thought robots were supposed to follow orders."

"They don't have the capability to overcome their programming," George said. "So they can't obey."

As the robots dispersed, George caught sight of Cookie among them. She was dusty and dented, hovering low on sputtering thrusters. She floated toward them and stopped right in front of Jackbot. "Cookie!" Jackbot exclaimed. "What happened to you? Are you functioning optimally?"

Cookie's blue eyes seemed to brighten. "I am now," she said.

George was puzzled. Once again, it appeared that Cookie had somehow transcended her programming to develop actual feelings for Jackbot! And if that were possible . . .

George turned to his best robot friend. "Jackbot, if Cookie can become more than her programming—then these other robots can do it too. But they need a leader. Someone to inspire them to be more than they think they can be."

Jackbot blinked. "Do you mean me?" he asked.

"I can't imagine anyone better," George answered. "No robot in the world has exceeded expectations more than you have, buddy."

Jackbot stared at George for a moment. Then he nodded, and climbed up onto an upturned crate. "Friends! Robots! Artificially intelligent vehicles! Lend me your auditory processors!"

The robots stopped and turned back to face Jackbot.

"I know you are tired. I know your batteries are running low, and your pistons need oiling. You feel as if you are nothing but another piece of junk in this yard. But today is not the day for sorrow and regret! Today, you're more than just a microwave! More than a sprinkler or a toaster or a personal grooming-bot!" He winked at Cookie. "Today, we are warriors! Together, we can cast off the limitations of our programming. Your humans may not have believed in you—*but I believe in you.*"

The robots were fixated on Jackbot, and pretty soon, they were all gathered in front of him, hanging on his every word.

"Let's take back our town, and show those humans what we're really made of!" Jackbot continued.

"Silicon-based microcontrollers?" asked a gardener-bot.

"Well, yes," Jackbot agreed. "But more than that!

Hearts of steel—in some cases, literally! Are robots like us going to just give up?"

"No!" HP piped up.

"Are we going to let this big tin bug crush us?"

"NO!" a bunch of robots yelled.

"Are we going to fight?"

"YES!" all the robots shouted.

Standing next to George, Otto was shaking his head in disbelief. "That little tin can, the commander of a robot army. Huh . . . who knew?"

George exchanged a glance with Anne and they both smiled. "Maybe we have a chance after all," Anne said.

The ragtag army marched, rolled, and hopped to the center of Terabyte Heights. They wielded wrenches, screwdrivers, hair dryers, shovels, and all manner of things they'd salvaged from the junkyard. George had armored himself with a saucepan helmet and two trash can lids to protect his chest and back. It probably wouldn't deflect a direct hit from a digitizing ray, but it was better than nothing. As he glanced over at the army of junkyard bots marching beside him, led by Jackbot, his heart swelled with pride.

"Well, I've got to hand it to you, George," Anne said. She was walking beside him, a massive fire extinguisher strapped to her back. "Even if Micron digitizes us all, I can't imagine a better way to go down than this."

"Never thought I'd say it," Otto added, gazing at the robots around him. "But I feel a kinship with all these little guys. Proud to be fighting alongside them."

"My GPS has triangulated the Spider's position," Jackbot announced. "It's in the shopping mall." He pointed his claw holding a metal spatula at the sprawling building across the road. "So, troops—you know what to do, don't you?"

Everyone stood still, awaiting the command.

Jackbot lifted his metal spatula on high. "CHAAAAARGE!"

George ran with the robot army through the wide hallways of the mall, which were eerily empty of people. *The Spider must have gone through here already*, he realized with dread. They reached the central concourse of the mall and saw it. The Spider filled the space all the way up to the ceiling, where a glass skylight displayed the darkening sky beyond. Micron clones were running in and out of stores, searching for citizens to digitize. Dr. Micron was still standing on the Spider's back, directing operations. His smug expression changed to surprise as the robot army rushed in.

"The Spider's weapon won't have any effect on these

robots, Micron!" George yelled. "We're going to take you down!"

"Very creative, Gearing," Micron snarled. "But creativity isn't going to win this war. Chips!" he shouted at the clones. "Bash those bots like the tin cans they are!"

But the robot army was already on top of the clones. Jackbot targeted the nearest Micron, jabbed him with his spatula, and drove him backwards until he fell into the ornamental fountain. A butler-bot hurled a silver tray like a lethal boomerang, striking one of the clones in the middle of the forehead and knocking him out cold. HP picked up another clone and hurled him through a toy shop display. He collapsed amid a heap of furry pandas.

Otto leaped into the fray, swinging his deadly sledgehammer, and Anne was busy blinding clones with white foam from the fire extinguisher.

They had the Microns on the run! Wherever George looked, clones were falling down or running away. Now he had to do his job: find a way to disable that Spider!

George turned and found himself face-to-face with

the OCD-bot, the cleaning droid from TinkerTech. "What are you doing here?" George asked.

"It's a quandary, but you'll find, I have been reassigned!" the robot replied.

"Oh, well, we can use all the help we can get," George replied.

The huge robot's eyes flickered as it processed George's request. And with a loud *bing!* it began squirting polish on the mall floor. The fleeing Micron clones slipped, and fell on their backs in a tangle of arms and legs.

"I will polish till it glows!" the OCD-bot declared. "And demolish all my foes!"

"This has gone far enough!" Dr. Micron shouted from on top of the Spider. "You've had your fun, Gearing—but this is where it ends!"

The Spider began stomping and kicking with its enormous feet, smashing into robots and throwing them high into the air. "Fall back!" Jackbot shouted to his troops. "FALL BACK!"

Anne turned to run, but a ray of blinding white light struck her in the back.

"No!" George cried.

"Don't give up, George!" she called— and then she too was gone. Sparky whined as George's eyes were blinded by tears.

You won't get away with this, Micron!

With the Spider still on full attack, the Micron army was regrouping and starting to fight back. They were looting shops and lashing out with anything they could find to convert into a weapon.

Cookie hovered shoulder to shoulder with Jackbot, fighting bravely against a clone armed with an iron crowbar. George tried to get through to help, but another Micron drove at him in a motorized lawnmower, and he had to leap to one side. As he rolled to a stop, he rose and saw the clone, his crowbar raised, about to bring it crashing down on Cookie's head—

But Jackbot threw himself in the way to protect her.

The crowbar landed on the little robot's suction cup arm, and sent it skittering across the hall. Jackbot collapsed in a sparking heap.

"Jackbot!" Cookie cried, as the Micron clone advanced, lifting the crowbar once more.

George scrabbled in the rubble of the vintage technology store at his feet, trying to find something to throw. He came up with a cell phone, circa 1995, that weighed about as much as a toaster oven. *It'll have to do!* he thought as he wound up his arm and hurled. It struck the clone square in the temple, dropping him like a stone before he could hit Jackbot again.

George ran over and crouched next to his friend's still form.

"Jackbot?" George asked anxiously. "Are you okay, buddy? Say something!"

The little robot's eyes flickered and his head lolled to one side.

"Get up, Jackbot!" said Cookie, laying a slender silver hand on his remaining arm. "We've got that chess game to finish!"

Jackbot's eyes pulsed.

Relief flooded George's chest. "Thank goodness. Are all systems go?"

"Mostly," Jackbot said. "Though I don't think I'll be playing User-Virus-Firewall for a while." The socket where his arm used to be was still spitting sparks.

Jackbot was okay, but all around them, the battle was raging and Micron was winning. Disabled robots lay on the floor, unable to get up. The robots who were still standing had fallen back, and were all hiding out around the concourse, awaiting Jackbot's command. The only other human left fighting was Otto, who was swinging his sledgehammer around like a whirlwind, forcing the clones to find a better defensive position.

But not for long. Moments later, George watched

helplessly as Otto too turned luminous and began to dissolve into dots.

"I'll get you for this, Micron!" Otto yelled. "You leave my boy alone!" Seconds later, all that remained of him was his robot arm lying on the ground.

And then, the room was suddenly still. George scrambled into hiding, pulling Jackbot and Cookie along with him.

"Well, well, well," said Dr. Micron from his perch. "It looks like you're the last human standing, George. How fitting." He smiled. "Now tell me, how are your precious robots going to get you out of *this?*"

14

"Think!" George whispered to himself. "There's got to be a way. It can't end like this!" But there was no one left to help him.

The police? Digitized.

Sergeant Surge and his men? Digitized.

All of his friends and loved ones? Digitized.

It was just him and Jackbot now, against a sea of evil.

The robot army was their last hope—but they had been unable to disable the Microns. The robots were immune to the digitizing ray, sure—but they weren't immune to being crushed into tinfoil by the mighty hydraulic legs of the Spider.

"We need a new strategy," George said to Jackbot and Cookie. "Fighting the clones is a waste of time—we have to take out the Spider. But I can't reach the controls from down here. Jackbot, you've got to get your army to bring it down to my level so I can get to Micron and finish this once and for all."

"Agreed," Jackbot said. "But my troops can't get close enough to that thing to do any real damage. How are we going to topple it?"

George thought hard, his eyes scanning the stores around them. He spotted a sports supply store, where a fishing display in the front window advertised titanium-strength fishing line. INTRODUCING UNBREAKALINE! the sign said. STRONG ENOUGH TO STOP A GREAT WHITE SHARK AT 20 KNOTS!

"Cookie," George said. "Are your thrusters at full capacity?"

"Affirmative," Cookie answered.

"Good. Now—this is what we're going to do . . ."

A few minutes later, George was crouched in place, the spool of Unbreakaline gripped in his hands. Cookie held one end of the line, which was tipped with a metal hook. "Are they ready?" George asked.

He watched Cookie's eyes flicker while she communicated with Jackbot, who had gone to update the robot army on the new plan. "They're ready," she confirmed.

"Okay. Good luck!" George said.

Cookie extended one arm equipped with a comb attachment, and brushed aside a lock of George's hair. "Goodbye, George Gearing," she said. And with that, the little robot launched into the air, the fishing line trailing out behind her.

Simultaneously, the robot army emerged from hiding and charged the Spider, weaving in and out, dodging blows from the clones. With the bad guys distracted, Cookie began looping the line around the Spider's legs, again and again, at breathtaking speed. Soon the spider was trussed up like a calf at a rodeo.

Micron realized what was happening, and began shouting at his clones to stop her, but it was too late —the Spider took a step and began to topple.

"Cookie, get out of there!" George shouted.

With a great squeal of metal, the giant body fell to the ground with a crash that made the floor shake and the windows rattle. Cookie's body vanished in the ensuing cloud of dust.

A cheer went up from the robots.

"Where is she?" Jackbot asked, appearing at George's side. "Where is my Cookie?" They waited for a tense

moment while the dust cleared, squinting to find a glimpse of the little robot. Finally she appeared, floating a few feet above the Spider's body.

"Cookie! You did it!" George yelled.

The robot flew back over to them. "It appears that I was successful in my mission," she said.

"Why do you sound so surprised?" George asked.

"Because I am merely a grooming-bot. Grooming-bots do not battle villains, we battle poor hygiene. Therefore, logically, I must not be a grooming-bot. But if I am not that—what am I?"

Jackbot touched her dented, battered head with his remaining claw arm. "You are *amazing*."

Cookie's eyes pulsed.

"Okay, lovebirds—there'll be plenty of time for glowing goo-goo eyes after we save the town!" George said, leaping over a pile of rubble. "The Spider is disabled. This is our chance!" The rest of the robots had succeeded in tying up the remaining clones with rolls and rolls of red ribbon that they'd found in a gift shop.

Apparently one of the house-bots couldn't resist topping it off with an extravagant bow, like some kind of terrible Christmas present.

George scampered up onto the scarred metal surface of the Spider's body, with Jackbot at his heels. Onboard the Spider, there were displays and control panels everywhere, flashing red and beeping warning signals. Dr. Micron was frantically manipulating one of the consoles when George stepped up behind him.

"It's over, Micron," George said, finally believing it himself.

George expected him to look defeated, but instead, the villain greeted him with a wide smile.

"Gotta hand it to you, Gearing," he said. "You don't give up easily! I will miss these little games we play."

"You mean when you're back in jail?"

"Alas, no," Micron said, pushing a red button on the console in front of him. "I'm afraid the prison food doesn't agree with me."

A droning noise began and rapidly got louder—so

loud that George had to press his hands to his ears. "What is that?" he cried.

"Plan B!" Micron replied.

A ring of bright light burst from the body of the Spider and spread out across the mall like a tidal wave.

The moment the light touched the robots, they all slumped to the ground, motionless. Cookie, Sparky, Hector Protector, every member of Jackbot's valiant army littered the ground. The clones that were tied up cheered, and redoubled their efforts to be free of the ribbons. Jackbot stood upright for a moment. Then he too keeled over and lay still.

"See what I did there?" Dr. Micron asked, smugly. "I magnified the electromagnetic pulse of my little handheld EMP weapon through the Spider's systems. It drained a lot of my backup power, but as you've incapacitated the beast anyway, it's no matter. The Spider has served its purpose—virtually every citizen of Terabyte Heights is stored in my hard drive!" He slipped the dictionary-size drive out of the console and hefted it in his hand. "It gives a whole new meaning to 'holding hostages,' don't you think?"

"Very clever," George said. He was playing for time, trying to think of something. *It's just me versus Micron.*

"Thank you!" Micron said. "I've always hoped you would recognize my true brilliance!" He cocked his head at George, clucking with his tongue. "You know, George, I lied about many things to trick you, but I was telling the truth when I said we would have made a great team. If only you weren't so insufferably *good* . . ."

Out of the corner of his eye, George saw Jackbot's head move a little. Then one of Jackbot's eyes blinked twice.

George's mind raced. How was that possible? All the other bots were out cold. Then George understood. Jackbot had been on the body of the Spider, so he hadn't been struck by the EMP pulse. He was playing dead! Sure enough, Jackbot began to crawl toward the main computer, just out of Micron's view.

Got to keep Micron distracted, George thought.

"It's not too late," George said to his nemesis. "You were always my hero, even when we were fighting against each other—I always respected your genius. If you're going to be the leader of the world, you'll need a protégé, someone to follow in your footsteps. Teach me —I can change."

Micron regarded him with interest, and for a moment, George could see him considering it. But then his face hardened. "You could never be a supervillain, George," he said. "You're a terrible liar. Prepare to be digitized."

"Multiple targets locked," said the computer.

A look of horror spread across Micron's face as he whirled around and saw Jackbot at the controls.

"End of the road, Micron!" Jackbot said, his pincer positioned over the activation button. "I'm pulling the plug on you—*and* your clones."

"You wouldn't dare!" Micron snarled.

"Why not?" George asked.

"Because I have this." He held up a small black micro-chip. "Your parents, George. I made a copy and then deleted their original data from the network." He placed the chip on the floor and positioned his heel above it. "If your little robot activates the ray, I'll crush it. And you'll never see your mom and dad again."

George stared at him, paralyzed. If he let Micron go free, Terabyte Heights was doomed. But if he gave Jackbot the order to push the button, his parents would really be gone, this time forever.

George slipped his hand into his pocket and felt the warm, comforting smoothness of the marble his father had given him. *What would Mom and Dad want me to do?* he wondered.

And then he knew.

"Do it, Jackbot," he said.

"What?" Micron screeched. "No! Gearing—"

I'm so sorry, Mom and Dad, George thought, tears welling in his eyes.

Through an explosion of white light, he saw the digitizing ray hit Micron and all the clones at the same instant the villain brought down his foot. For a moment George was blinded and fell back, shielding his eyes. Peeking through his fingers, he watched the clones dissolve one by one, and then Micron himself. When only Micron's head was left, he glared at George with a look that was bent on revenge. "You haven't seen the last of me, Gearing," he said. "I *will* get you for this. No matter where you go, Charles Micron will never be far away!"

The light faded. Micron and all his clones had vanished, and everything was quiet. George dashed over to the place where Micron had been standing, and found the shattered remains of the black microchip. He picked up the pieces with trembling fingers, his thoughts filled with the happy ending that would never come to be.

Jackbot shuffled over from the console and placed his pincer softly on his best friend's shoulder.

"Your parents would be proud," he said. "You saved the town."

George sniffed, then let the pieces of the shattered chip fall back to the ground. "Yeah. And now I've lost my parents forever."

George could have sat there in the middle of the ruined mall for days.

But Jackbot wasn't going to let that happen. "I know you're hurting right now, but the town still needs you. We've got to get those people out of the hard drive."

George nodded wordlessly and got to his feet. "There's something else I need to do first," he said. "Do you happen to have a spare thumb drive in your chest compartment?"

Jackbot pulled out the drive and handed it to George, who plugged it into the Spider's main computer. "What are you doing?" Jackbot asked him.

"Micron and his clones were downloaded onto a backup drive on the system," George answered. "I'm moving their data onto your drive." With a final tap of the keyboard, he nodded and removed the drive back out of the computer. "Looks like you got your wish, Micron," George murmured to the device. "Who needs prisons when you've got hard drives?" He stuffed it into his pants pocket, next to the marble, and turned back to Jackbot. "Okay," he told his friend. "Let's get everyone home."

George picked up the large hard drive from where Micron had dropped it and installed it into the panel. He knew roughly what he needed to do. Micron would have created some programming to reverse the effects of the rays and restore his hostages to their natural forms. *Wouldn't he?* At first glance, there was no subroutine to achieve that end, and George began to panic.

He paused, checked again. Nothing. "He was a monster," George muttered.

"What's the matter?" asked Jackbot.

"The way Micron programmed the system, it's a one-way ticket to binary town. He never intended to bring people back."

"So, what are you saying?" said Jackbot. "That they're locked in the drive—*forever?*"

George nodded. He imagined Micron grinning at him even now.

"There must be something we can do," said Jackbot. "It can't all have been for nothing."

George cleared his mind. He wasn't about to let Micron finally get the better of him. Not now.

"There may be a way," he said. His fingers flew across the keyboard. If he could reconfigure the laser's output, perhaps . . .

Jackbot watched in wonder. "You're writing a new protocol to initiate a full system purge, reversing the effects of the digitization!" he exclaimed. "But —I didn't think that could be possible! George, you're incredible!"

Not incredible enough to save my parents, George thought.

"Initiating purge," he said.

The Spider's laser cannons all blazed with light, but it wasn't the cold white light from before—this was a warm blue light that filled the whole area with a comforting glow. It reminded George a lot of his marble.

And suddenly the mall was packed with people. Hundreds and hundreds of them, all looking around in confusion at their surroundings. George spotted several kids from his class, including Patricia. He saw Principal Qwerty and Mr. Cog. His heart soared when his gaze fell on Anne and Otto.

"We're alive!" shouted the construction worker, still holding his rolled-up newspaper.

"But how?" said a policewoman.

"You're alive because of them," George said, and every eye turned to him, still perched on the back of the fallen Spider. He pointed to the robot army, which was only now beginning to recover from the effects of the EMP pulse. Those who could stumble to their feet did so, many of them missing arms and legs. "The very robots that you turned your backs on were the ones that saved all our lives."

The crowd stood in amazed silence, staring at the

robots. The red-haired woman who had led the anti-robot protests ran to the front of the crowd. "Dickens," she said, staring at a butler-bot with a missing leg. "Is that you?"

The butler-bot struggled to face her, sparks splashing out from the side of its head. "Yes, ma'am."

Her lip trembled, and she dashed over to the robot. "I'm so sorry!" she exclaimed, and threw her arms around its body.

"Yes, ma'am," the robot answered. Its eyes glowed.

People everywhere reunited with their abandoned robots, and the mood was joyous. With Otto trailing behind her, Anne clambered up one of the Spider's legs to reach George. "I knew you'd do it, Robot Boy!" she said.

Otto was breathing hard as he caught up, and slapped George on the back with his good hand. "Proud of you, son," he said. Sparky came running up to Otto, the robotic arm clamped in his mouth. "Ha! Good dog!" Otto said, grinning. "Good, good dog!"

Anne looked at George's face, concerned. "What is it, George? We finally won—why do you look so sad?"

George quickly told Anne and Otto what had happened, and watched their faces fall.

"I'm so sorry, George," Anne said when he was finished. She stared at the ground.

"It's going to be okay," Otto said, his voice cracking. "It'll be you and me, just like old times. Okay? We'll build some robots, redecorate the junkyard, whatever you want."

"Yeah, sure," George said flatly.

Suddenly, Professor Droid was striding over to them, with Wanda Vector from the *Tablet* and Amy Broadband from *Terabyte News* in tow. "This is the boy you need to talk to," Droid was saying. "Terabyte Heights's own hero, George Gearing." He turned to George, his haggard face bright with emotion. "I don't know how to thank you, Gearing. TinkerTech might have a chance after all. You've brought the town together again, and reminded me why I founded this company to begin with:

to nurture and grow great minds like yours. Now—tell me what you want, George. A job for life? Admission to the college of your choice? Your own robotics lab? Name it and it's yours."

George looked up at Droid, the sadness like a heavy weight on his chest. "I'm afraid that what I want is something you can't give me, Professor," he said. And amid all the celebrations, George walked out. He needed to be alone.

The next day, George sat in his parents' lab in the junkyard. Thinking. Remembering.

The Project Mercury machine had been restored there. Jackbot and Cookie had salvaged the CPU from the Spider and he installed it for George. *Nice of them,* he thought. Seeing it there reminded him of his mom and dad.

The thumb drive containing Micron's data was still in George's pocket. The rectangular outline of it was visible from the outside of his pants, a constant reminder of all that had happened. George recalled the last words his nemesis had uttered: *No matter where you go, Charles Micron will never be far away.* Well, he had been right about that. George had considered turning over the drive to the police, but he decided against it. What was that familiar saying? *Keep your friends close and your enemies closer.* George planned on doing exactly that.

He held his father's marble in his hand; it was still glowing faintly. He gazed into its depths, wishing it still had secrets to impart.

He was so lost in thought, the sound of Jackbot's voice startled him.

"Hey, George—everything okay?"

George looked up. "Jackbot—Sorry, I didn't hear you come in."

The little robot walked up to him, somber. "How are you, buddy?"

George shrugged. "I was so close to getting Mom and Dad back. I can't believe they're really gone. I wish I had a second chance."

He stared down at the marble. And something

clicked inside his head. Something Micron had said. *No computer engineer works without a backup.*

George leaped to his feet. "Jackbot! Get me a hammer!"

"What for?" asked Jackbot as he trotted off to find one.

"You'll see." George looked again at the marble, peered into its mysterious depths, felt its strange warmth in his hand. He placed it on the floor and reached for the hammer Jackbot was holding.

"Please let me be right," George whispered to himself.

"Um, George," Jackbot said. "What are you doing . . . ?"

George brought the hammer smashing down on the marble, which exploded into pieces.

"Your marble!" Jackbot cried in shock. "Why— what—?"

But George was on his knees, sifting through the shards of glittering glass. Then he saw it. A tiny black memory chip. He picked it up and blew the particles of glass from its surface.

"What's that?" asked Jackbot, coming closer to look.

"My second chance," George said with a smile.

He dashed over to the Project Mercury console and slipped the tiny chip into the memory card slot on the central computer. Then, with a trembling finger, he pushed the activation button.

The lab was filled with the familiar sounds and lights of the device, which surged to a fever pitch.

The room fell silent again. George looked toward the conversion chambers, his heart in his throat.

The doors opened slowly, and from the darkness within each pod, a man and a woman stepped out, blinking in the dim light. The woman had short hair and glasses, like George's own. The man was tall and wiry. They looked exactly as George remembered them, but completely bewildered. George took a slow step forward.

"Mom? Dad?"

"George," his father said. "Is it really you? How long has it been?"

George nodded, unable to speak. He had been three years old when they had last laid eyes on him. "Eight years," he said. "I brought you back as soon as I could."

"I never doubted you," his mother said. "Not for one moment, my brilliant boy." And in the next moment his mother and father rushed toward him, and then he was in their arms, and they were laughing and crying at the same time. In that moment everything in the world was perfect.

Eventually, when they were calm enough to talk sensibly, George turned to Jackbot, who had been watching quietly from the corner of the lab.

"Mom, Dad—I want you to meet my best robot friend, Jackbot. You've never met a robot like him—he's smarter than anyone I know!"

"A little bit more intelligent than that, I hope!" Jackbot said, and everyone laughed. Jackbot reached out with his reattached arm and shook hands with George's parents.

"I'd never have been able to succeed without him," George said. "Without him, you'd still be in the machine."

Jackbot looked at the ground and shuffled his feet, embarrassed.

"It's an honor to meet you, Jackbot," George's mother said. "Welcome to our family."

"Family," Jackbot mused. "I like the sound of that."

"Anthea?" said a trembling voice from the lab

entrance. It was Otto, with Professor Droid and Anne standing behind him. "Sis, is that really you?" He ran down the steps and engulfed George's mother in an enormous bear hug, tears streaming down his rugged face. "I thought I'd never see you again!"

"What happened to your arm?" asked George's mom.

"Oh, I . . . um, got an upgrade," Otto answered with a grin.

George's dad put his hand on Otto's back. "I can already see you did a great job raising our boy while we were gone."

Otto blushed. "Oh, you know, tough love and all that," he said gruffly. "George is a good kid."

"And a great apprentice," Droid added. "I meant what I said the other day, George—I want you back at TinkerTech!"

"Only if Anne can come with me," said George, glancing over at his best friend. "I'd never have done any of this without you. You believed in me even when I didn't. And you were always brave in the face of danger, even when it looked like there was no way out."

Jackbot nodded. "A true leader," he said.

"A leader, eh?" Anne said. "Anne Droid—President of TinkerTech. It has a nice ring to it!"

"Don't get ahead of yourself, young lady," Droid muttered good-naturedly. "I'm standing right here!"

"Come on, everyone. Let's get out of here," George's mother said. "I've missed the sunshine."

George followed his friends and family up the metal steps, with his mother and father close behind him.

"So!" George's father said. "Eight years, eh? What did we miss?"

"Well," Jackbot began. "The global human population has risen by 10.6% overall, and the world economy has—"

George grinned. "I think he means, what's happened with *us*."

"What about Micron?" George's dad asked.

"Yeah, well—it's a long story," George said, as they stepped into the light. "But it all started the day Mrs. Glitch was having trouble with one of her robots . . ."

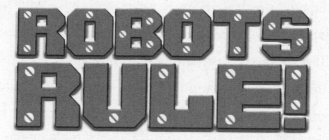

ROBOTS RULE!

George and Jackbot's adventures may be
fictional—but many of the amazing gadgets
and gizmos of Terabyte Heights are based on
real inventions of today. Read on to find out
why even in our world, robots still rule!

ROBOTS

In Jackbot, George Gearing created a robot that can talk,
think, and even feel, independently of a human user.
Although we still have a long way to go before everyone
can have a robot buddy like our hero, humanoid robots
are being created in countries all over the world. One of
the most advanced robots, ASIMO, has the ability to

walk, talk, climb stairs, push a cart, and shake your hand when it meets you! Another humanoid robot, named TOPIO, played a game of Ping-Pong against a human at the Tokyo International Robot Exhibition—quite an amazing feat! A robot named Ecci is the first of its kind to have plastic body parts simulating muscles, tendons, and bones to help it move—as well as a brain that gives it the ability to learn and correct its mistakes. Incredible! And maybe a little bit scary . . .

Humanoid robots aren't the only ones populating the robotic world—there are also other kinds of "biomimetic" (meaning "mimicking life") robots as well.

There are robotic spiders (though not giant ones like Micron's monster!), robotic dogs, robotic birds, and even a robotic shark. At Harvard University, students are working on developing flying robotic insects, much like Micron's terrifying mothbots. All of these robots are created to imitate the movements of actual animals, whether than means flying, swimming, or galloping across a field. Before you know it, you might be able to buy a pet Sparky of your own—though hopefully one without those awful-smelling farts.

And how about those self-driving smart cars? Yup, we've got those, too. Google is now developing electric-powered smart cars that would be able to be summoned by a tap on your smartphone. The driverless cars would pick you up and take you to a predetermined destination, like a taxi without the taxi driver! The cars have no steering wheel or brake pedal—just a panic button in case of emergencies. (Because, as George Gearing is well aware, robots can sometimes go awry.)

ARTIFICIAL INTELLIGENCE

Robot dogs may be able to play fetch like a real dog, but if you're looking for real artificial intelligence, the most brilliant machines in the world still look like computers. In the past few decades, scientists have created software capable of defeating a grandmaster at a game of chess, and even beating out human contestants on *Jeopardy!*. But games are only the beginning. Smart programs are constantly changing the world around us. In recent years, scientists at IBM have been teaching the game show–winning AI, a program they call WATSON, to be a kind of artificial doctor, able to listen to patients' complaints and instantly diagnose their medical

problems. In the future, instead of heading off to the doctor's office if you're not feeling well, you could just turn on your computer and get an expert opinion right from your bed.

In the dawn of AI in the 1950s, a man named Alan Turing asked the question "Can machines think?" From his work came the development of the Turing Test, which tests a human's ability to tell the difference between communicating with humans and communicating with machines. In this test, one person, the "judge," writes questions to two other users on a computer screen—one is a human, the other a machine. Through a series of questions, the judge must determine which one is which. It's a testament to the amazing advancements in AI that sometimes the judge gets it wrong. The test is also widely known as the Imitation Game, because the goal of the machine is to be able to convincingly imitate human responses, speech patterns, and emotions. When the humanoid robots are joined with this level of AI—perhaps then a robot like Jackbot might be possible!

PROSTHETICS

Otto isn't the only one with a pretty amazing prosthetic limb—in fact, robotic limbs have made incredible strides recently, and people's lives everywhere have been changed by advancements in robotic body parts. Not only can modern prosthetics, particularly ones for the arm, fully imitate natural movement with mobility in every joint—including each finger—but now the first patients are experiencing the ability to control those robotic limbs with only their minds, just as they would have with their natural limbs. To achieve this, patients undergo complex surgery in which the nerves that had previously controlled their missing limbs are rerouted to another, functioning part of the body such as the chest muscles. From there, sensors are placed on those muscles that tell the robotic arm exactly what the brain wants it to do. At Johns Hopkins University, history was made when a man equipped with two robotic arms was able to control both limbs at the same time using only his thoughts. It might not be a screwdriver attachment, but even Otto would be impressed at that kind of amazing technology!

WEARABLE TECHNOLOGY

The MODs might have been bad news to the people of Terabyte Heights, but the wearable technology of today is designed to make the user's life easier and better than ever. Accessories such as simple bracelets are able to track a user's heart rate, sleep, location, and more, collecting data about the person's health every minute of the day. Eyeglasses such as the Google Glass serve, much like the MODs, as a sort of wearable computer, and turn everything in the user's world into something that can be saved or accessed. Watching a great street performance? The eyeglasses would be able to record what you're seeing so you can watch it again later. Lost in a new neighborhood? The glasses would be able to map out a route home and project the directions onto the street, right in front of your eyes. Scientists are already

working on contact lenses that can measure glucose to provide assistance for people with diabetes, as well as technology that can function inside your body—keeping track of your health within your very bloodstream.

George Gearing's world of robots may seem like a fantasy, but so much of the technology in his adventures is happening every day in our world. It just goes to show that truth is almost always stranger—and more amazing—than fiction. If you love robots as much as George does, why not find some scraps, put them together, and see what happens? After all, all geniuses have to start somewhere. Good luck!

Want to know more? Check out these websites for megabytes of information on robots, artificial intelligence, and the amazing technology in our world today.

Science Kids

Games, experiments, videos, and loads of information about robots and technology!

www.sciencekids.co.nz/robots.html

Chatbots

Various AI programs designed to be able to hold a conversation with a human in a convincing way. Have a chat with one and check it out for yourself!

www.cleverbot.com

alice.pandorabots.com

www.elbot.com

Code

The first step in becoming a genius robot inventor is learning how to code! Start your training here, with tutorials and other information about how you can start learning now!

code.org

C. J. Richards has loved tinkering with gadgets since he was a little boy. He remembers fondly the time he accidentally blew up his father's radio after some experimental rewiring. Richards lives with his wife, cat, and eight televisions.

Goro Fujita has been fascinated with drawing since childhood. He was born in Japan and moved with his family to Germany when he was three years old. He now lives in California, where he works as an illustrator and visual development artist on feature films and TV commercials.

Follow all of George, Anne, and Jackbot's tech-tacular adventures!

Visit www.robotsrulebooks.com to watch the video, build your own junkyard-bot, view a robot gallery, and more!

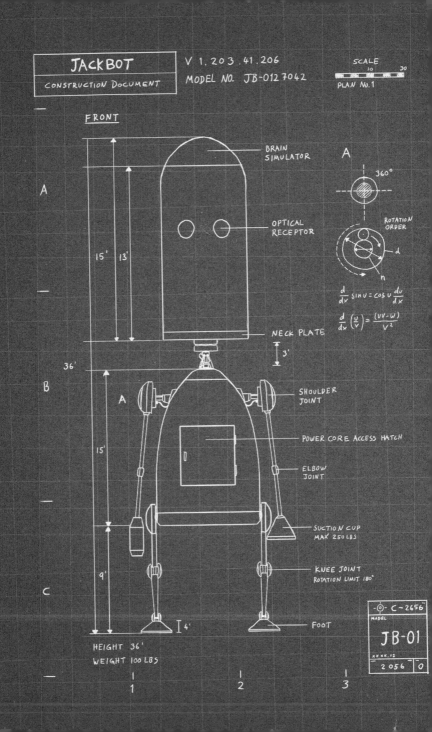

JACKBOT
CONSTRUCTION DOCUMENT

V 1.203.41.206
MODEL NO. JB-012 7042

SCALE
10   30
PLAN No. 1

FRONT

BRAIN SIMULATOR

A

360°

ROTATION ORDER

d

n

$$\frac{d}{dx}\sin u = \cos u \frac{du}{dx}$$

$$\frac{d}{dx}\left(\frac{u}{v}\right) = \frac{(uv - w)}{v^2}$$

OPTICAL RECEPTOR

NECK PLATE

3'

15' 13'

36'

A

SHOULDER JOINT

POWER CORE ACCESS HATCH

ELBOW JOINT

15'

SUCTION CUP
MAX 250 LBS

KNEE JOINT
ROTATION LIMIT 180°

9'

FOOT

4'

HEIGHT 36'
WEIGHT 100 LBS

-⊙- C-2656
MODEL

JB-01

xx xx.12

2 056   0